CORVUS

OATH OF VENGEANCE

CORVUS

OATH OF VENGEANCE

JAMES THOMSON

BOXER BOOKS

First published in Great Britain in 2010
by Boxer Books Limited.
www.boxerbooks.com

ISBN 978-1-907152-41-2

1 3 5 7 9 10 8 6 4 2

Printed in Great Britain

All of our papers are sourced from managed forests
and renewable resources.

James Thomson is a writer and games designer. He is the author of over 20 books for children and has also written for radio and television. He loves playing computer games, reading historical and science fiction novels, watching films and going for long walks. He lives in Sussex, in the land of the South Saxons.

Contents

Cast of characters

ALDFRID

One of a pair of hunter brothers from Mercia. His name means something like 'ancient peace'.

ALDHELM

Aldfird's brother. His name means 'ancient protector' in Anglo-Saxon.

CEARL

Saxon chief of the village of Wotanhirst.

CORVUS

The name of our hero. In Latin it means 'raven'. Corvus' mother, a Christian from southern Europe and a Latin speaker, named him Corvus. As the raven is also a sacred bird to the Vikings, his Norse father was happy with the name.

DAGOBERT

A Frankish merchant. The name means something like 'good and bright'.

DROGO

One of Sighere's retainers. The name can mean 'ghost' or 'phantom' in Old English.

EDRIC GODWYN

The Saxon king's champion. He is of the Godwyn family, which eventually gave rise to King Harold, who died at Hastings. Edric means 'rich ruler' in Anglo-Saxon.

FREIA

One of Corvus' sisters. Named for the Norse goddess of love.

GUNNAR HALLESON

Corvus' father, Gunnar, son of Halle (Corvus' grandfather). Gunnar means 'war warrior' in Old Norse.

HENGIST

A Saxon warrior, father of Merewyn. His name means 'stallion' in Anglo-Saxon.

HILDR
Wulfric's wife. The name means something like 'battle' in Old Norse. Nice name for a wife, eh?

HORSA
Cearl's son. The name actually does mean 'horse' in Anglo-Saxon.

INGRID
One of Corvus' kidnapped sisters. Her name means something like 'god's beauty' in Old Norse.

KELDA
Wulfric's mother. Many say that she is a witch. In Old Norse, Kelda means 'fountain', 'spring' or 'well'.

LARS SILKBEARD
One of Wulfric's captains and a high-ranking Slaughter Wolf.

MEREWYN
This name predates the Saxons and is of Welsh origin. It probably means 'sea maiden'.

Orm the Old

An old friend of Corvus. Orm means 'snake' or 'dragon' in Old Norse.

Oslac, King of the South Saxons

There was a real ruler of Sussex called Oslac, but little is known about him.

Ragnar Oath-breaker

One of the Slaughter Wolves, and not to be trusted, as one can tell from his nickname... Ragnar means 'wise warrior' in Old Norse.

Sighere the Bald

Nephew of King Oslac and heir to the throne of the land of the South Saxons. His name means 'victorious army' in Old Saxon.

The Standard-Bearer

A mysterious figure who serves in Wulfric Cold-blood's force of Viking raiders, the Slaughter Wolves, as the standard-bearer. No one knows his real name.

WULFRIC COLD-BLOOD
Murderer of Corvus' parents. Kidnapper of his sisters. Chief of the Viking raiders, the Slaughter Wolves. His name means 'wolf power' or 'wolf ruler'.

WULFRIC 'JUNIOR'
A little boy, son of Wulfric Cold-blood.

CHAPTER 1

OATH OF VENGEANCE

*C*orvus rounded a bend in the trail and skidded to a halt. Two guards stood at ease by the wooden gate in front of Wulfric's Hall. Drawing his axes, Corvus ran straight at them. The guards were unprepared. They stood there for a moment, stunned.

Crash! The first guard went down, unconscious from a single axe strike to his helmeted head. The second only just had time to draw his sword and shoulder his shield before Corvus was upon him, bringing one axe down on the shield with such force that the bronze-rimmed wood split in half. A half-second later, he'd hooked the other axe around the man's ankle and pulled, toppling him over. Before he'd even hit the ground, Corvus had knocked him out with a single blow.

Neither guard had managed to utter a single word.

Corvus ran on into the compound, blue eyes blazing under a crown of long, shaggy, black hair. He came into a wide courtyard, enclosed by a wooden stockade. Several farm buildings were scattered near the fence. In the centre rose a large hall, shaped like an inverted Viking longboat with twin dragon prows rising up from either side of the doors, poised as if to strike at any unwanted visitor. Corvus was an unwanted visitor, that much was for sure...

The commotion at the gate had roused the inhabitants of the hall, and a large man came racing out of the wooden doors. At the sight of Corvus, he stopped, but not for long. Grabbing a spear from a stack of weapons by the door, he charged straight at Corvus, screaming a battle cry: "Slaughter, slaughter!"

Corvus was unimpressed. He sidestepped, deftly

avoiding the thrusting spear, which just missed his belly. Capitalising on his forward momentum, Corvus wheeled into the air once more, bringing both axes down on the spearman's helmeted head, sending him sprawling to the ground. Corvus had hardly broken his stride. As he ran forward, another of Wulfric's men emerged and stood, frozen in fear at the sight of Corvus' battle-skill. Corvus stood tall and roared at him. The man dropped his spear and ran. Corvus grinned, but soon his expression changed to a scowl. Why weren't there more guards? Corvus was ready to fight a hundred men! And where, by Odin's fury, was Wulfric?

The gutless coward must be hiding, thought Corvus. With only revenge on his mind, he dashed up the low wooden steps leading into the great hall. The dragon prows on either side of the doors seemed to glare at him in outrage. He stopped and stared at them for a moment, the hairs on the back of his neck bristling. Then, with one eye on the dragons, Corvus lifted a booted foot and kicked open the wooden doors. They burst inward with a loud crack, splintering into matchwood. With a final glance at the dragon heads, he ran inside, axes at the ready, then came to a stop, scowling. Where was Wulfric, by the sleet-cold halls of Hel?

Ahead, on a finely carved wooden throne studded with gems, sat an old woman. Behind her, a young woman held her stripling son close, clearly terrified. The boy was scowling angrily; the old woman seemed calm and resigned.

"Where is Wulfric?" bellowed Corvus.

The old woman rose slowly to her feet.

"Who are you?" she said haughtily. "How dare you enter this hall unbidden, with murder in your eyes?"

"Murder? This is not murder, this is vengeance! Do you not know who I am? I am Corvus Gunnarson, son of Gunnar Halleson, and I have sworn an oath by Odin All-father and Ullr, god of the blood feud, against that murdering villain Wulfric!"

As he said this, Corvus lifted his axes above his head. The weapons were well honed and deadly, and his wrath-twisted face made him look like a demon from the underworld of the White Christ.

At the sound of Corvus' name, the old woman blanched, and the young mother began to sob. They knew why he was here now, and, by the look of him, they were certain their death-day was upon them. Suddenly the boy broke free from his mother's arms. He dashed straight at Corvus, wielding a small sword that seemed almost a toy, save for its razored edge and needle-sharp point. The young mother screamed, "Wulfric, no!"

Corvus stepped back, surprised. He had to admire the boy's courage, even if he was obviously the son of Wulfric Cold-blood, the man he had sworn to kill. As the lad closed in, Corvus reversed his axe, so as not to draw blood, and swept it across the boy's path, knocking his feet from under him. He then placed a booted foot on the lad's chest, pinning him to the ground. Leaning down, he let forth his most ferocious snarl, deep and fearsome, right into the boy's face. The lad's courage gave out, and he quailed.

"Please," the boy's mother begged, taking a step forward. "Please don't kill my son!"

Then the old woman said, "We thought you were dead, Corvus Gunnarson."

"Ah, so that's why Wulfric killed my parents and burnt my father's homestead not two weeks ago! He thought I was dead – that there'd be no one to come back, eh? The gutless coward!"

"They've always hated each other, Gunnar and Wulfric," said the old woman, her eyes flicking from the struggling boy to Corvus' raised axe and back again.

"That's true, but Wulfric didn't have to kill him," said Corvus, his voice tense, full of barely suppressed anger.

The old woman said, "They'd been feuding for years; one of them was bound to die."

Corvus had to agree with that. Viking feuds were always bloody, and the feud between Wulfric and his father had lasted as long as he could remember. But then he smiled, a chilling sight.

"But Wulfric didn't have to kill my mother as well, did he?" he said, his voice ominously quiet. "He didn't have to take my sisters."

For a moment, there was silence. The old woman

stared at the floor. She knew Corvus' oath of vengeance was justified, according to the Old Ways. Wulfric had gone too far, and now his family would have to face the consequences.

"You're Kelda, aren't you, Wulfric Cold-blood's mother?" said Corvus.

The old woman went pale. "That I am." She took a step forward. "Take me, and spare my grandson," she said, holding up her head.

Corvus raised an eyebrow. Brave words, he had to admit.

"And that's his wife, Hildr, is it not?" said Corvus, pointing an axe at the young mother, who was wringing her hands, silently begging him to spare the boy.

"Aye, it is," said Kelda.

Suddenly Corvus felt a sharp sting of red-hot agony in his calf. The boy had stabbed him in the leg with his sword!

"Ow!" yelled Corvus, and he brought his axe hurtling down.

"No!" cried Kelda and Hildr in unison.

But Corvus' axe crashed into the wooden plank

near the lad's head. Wood chips sprayed across the floor, one of them drawing a bloody scratch along the boy's cheek. The boy looked aghast at Corvus, suddenly terrified. He started crawling backwards, as fast as he could, trying to get away from the vengeful Viking. Corvus straightened. The anger drained from his face.

"Bah, I do not make war on women and children!" he said. "I am not Wulfric."

The boy stood and ran into his mother's arms, staring back at Corvus with fear and hatred. Kelda and Hildr exchanged a look of relief. Maybe today would not be their death-day after all.

"Where are my sisters, Ingrid and Freia? And where is Wulfric?" demanded Corvus.

Kelda frowned and shook her head, signalling to Hildr that she should not tell. Corvus growled, a sound full of threat.

"He has taken them to England!" Hildr blurted out suddenly. "Just days ago."

"What? Why?" said Corvus.

Kelda glared at Hildr to shut up, but Hildr was having none of it. Wulfric was a pig; he had always been a pig, in fact, and she'd never wanted to marry him in the first place. All she cared about was her child. If telling Corvus what he wanted to know would keep her son out of danger, then so be it.

"He means to sell them," she continued. "He and his war band, the Slaughter Wolves, have built a settlement in the land of the South Saxons, and Wulfric has paid for his piece of earth with gold and slaves taken from the raids here in our own lands. The Saxons do not yet realise what a viper they have allowed into their midst. Your sisters are part of the final payment for that land."

Corvus narrowed his eyes in anger. His sisters. Slaves? Oh, how Wulfric would pay. He would pay in blood and gold, he would pay with his life.

Corvus took a menacing step forward. "If you lie..." he said.

"No, it is the truth! I swear it by Odin, and the White Christ!" said Hildr.

Corvus nodded, convinced. Such oaths were not to be taken lightly. "I will go to England."

With that he turned and walked out of Wulfric's hall, leaving Hilda, Kelda and young Wulfric shocked and scared, but glad to be alive. Corvus didn't see the glint of sour malice in Wulfric's mother's eyes as she glared at the back of Corvus' head, fingering the old bone necklace she wore around her neck and muttering under her breath.

As Corvus stepped over the splintered wreckage of the doors, he had a thought. It was obvious Hildr had little love for Wulfric. Maybe he hadn't really needed to charge in like that. Maybe if he'd just asked politely... Corvus shrugged. The event was in the past now, and there was no point spending too much time dwelling on it.

Outside he saw the young warrior who'd fled earlier, standing fully armed by the main gate.

"So, you've changed your mind, have you?" said Corvus, and without further ado he strode towards him purposefully, twirling his twin axes like juggler's clubs. The young man went pale and moved aside, his new-found courage dissolved.

Corvus gestured with his axe. The young man stepped further back, well away from the gate, and laid his spear and shield on the ground. Corvus nodded, and continued on and out of Wulfric's homestead. There was no point in killing people just because you could.

Corvus headed for a path that led to the seashore. He would go and see the fisherman, Orm the Old. Orm had a boat, and had been a friend to his father for many years. As he paced, his left boot began to make an unpleasant squelching sound. Looking down, he saw it was soaked in blood, thanks to Wulfric's boy, the god-cursed little dwarf. Brave, though, to stab a full-grown warrior. Corvus felt a twinge of guilt. He'd terrified the life out of that boy. You shouldn't do that to children or women – honour demanded it. That was what his father had taught him, and that's what he'd learnt at the court of the Danish King Godfred, where he'd spent the last five years in service in his royal bodyguard. On the other hand, the little boy had given as good as he'd got, if not better, Corvus thought, smiling wryly to himself.

Corvus stopped by the side of the path and removed his boot. He drew bandages, needle and thread from his belt-pouch, then cleaned and stitched the wound. Though he grimaced against the pain, he uttered not a sound. When he was finished, he strode on, as if it was nothing. It *was* nothing, just another wound, one of many to come, no doubt.

He made his way to Orm's hut on the seashore, where he found the old fisherman dragging a net from a single-masted fishing boat drawn up on the beach. He grinned when he saw Corvus approaching.

"Corvus 'Twin-axe' Gunnarson, by Thor!" said Orm, his weather-beaten face browned and wrinkled by years on the sea. "We thought you were dead – we got word that a Gunnarson had been killed at the battle of Lokr's Keep. As you were serving the king of Denmark, naturally we assumed it was you."

"Ah, now I see why everyone thinks I'm dead," said Corvus. "Actually, the Gunnarson that was killed at the battle was Karfves 'Blood-axe' Gunnarson, from Gotland, not me. We weren't even related."

"That's good news, then!" said Orm. "Well, not from Karfves' point of view, though," and he laughed. Then his face clouded. "You've heard about your parents, have you?"

"Aye, and seen the homestead as well. Wulfric will pay, I'll see to that," said Corvus. "I've just been looking for him but he was nowhere to be seen." His eyes narrowed in anger, and he gripped the hammer-shaped talisman he wore around his neck. "I've sworn an oath of vengeance."

Orm nodded. That was the honourable thing for Corvus to do, and only to be expected. He'd known the lad from when he was young – always fighting, exploring and having adventures. He'd only been twelve when he'd gone off to serve the king of the Danes in payment of a blood debt that his father had owed to King Godfred. Five years' service in the king's personal bodyguard, and now he was back, no longer a lad but a full-grown man. Corvus was seventeen years old and undoubtedly believed the world was there for the taking, that he was invincible, unstoppable. His reputation with the twin axes had reached his homelands some time ago. Well, thought Orm, if there was going to be a seventeen-year-old who was invincible and unstoppable, it would be Corvus. Only time would tell if he had his father's wisdom as well.

"Wulfric's gone to England with his war band, the Slaughter Wolves, and he's taken your sisters with him, to sell to the Saxons," said Orm.

"Aye, I know." Corvus felt a momentary twinge of guilt. He hadn't thought to ask Orm where Wulfric was. If he'd asked him first, there would have been no need to go up to Wulfric's hall. He'd scared those women to death, as well as the boy. Maybe he should have planned it all a bit better. He'd been so full of rage he hadn't really stopped to think. Seeing his family's burnt-out home had driven him over the edge.

But that was done. Now he had to hunt down that cruel murdering cur, Wulfric Cold-blood, and rescue his beloved sisters. Family was family and there was no one else but him. He would save them or die trying.

Corvus stepped up and put a hand on the old fisherman's shoulder. "Will you take me to England in your boat, Orm?" he asked.

CHAPTER 2

KELDA'S CURSE

Orm had agreed readily enough to the journey, but it would be a few days before the *Wind-weaver*, his fishing boat, was caulked and shipshape. Orm's boat was similar to the knarr – a single-masted sailing ship, usually used for trading and transport, and not to be confused with the longship, the dragon-prowed warship of the feared Viking reavers. Orm's boat was much smaller than a regular knarr and designed primarily for fishing, often with a single crewman.

Normally, if you were sailing to England, you'd follow the coastline past Denmark, Frisia and the kingdom of the Franks before hopping across the Channel. That was the safest way, but it took a long time. Corvus was in a hurry, so he'd managed to persuade Orm to take the direct route across the North Sea. His boat wasn't ideal for such a trip, but it was safe enough if the weather held.

That night, huddled in Orm's hut by the shore, they discussed the matter over a horn of ale and a bowl of fish broth.

"*Wind-weaver* is rather a grand name for a fishing boat," said Corvus.

Orm looked at him drily and raised an eyebrow, as if Corvus was some kind of fool. "It's what the Vanir call the heavens," he said.

"The Vanir? The old gods, you mean? They call the sky Wind-weaver?"

"Aye, they do," said Orm, sipping a spoonful of fish broth.

"So why name your boat after it?" said Corvus.

"In honour of Njord of the Vanir, god of the sea, sailors and fisherman. Every time Njord feels my boat on his skin, he will think of the sky. All things love the sky, even the gods," said Orm, staring at Corvus strangely, as if his mind was walking through the realm of the spirits even as he spoke.

Corvus shivered. He feared no man, no thing of flesh and blood. He'd always been like that, even as a boy. Others called him reckless, a trait his instructors in the bodyguard of the king of Denmark had tried to train out of him, with only partial success. Only the unknown world of the gods, spirits and magic scared him. Corvus thought perhaps all those years alone in a boat with only the sea-folk to talk with had touched Orm in the head, had brought him closer to the world of the spirits.

Corvus grasped the hammer-shaped amulet he wore around his neck. It represented Mjolnir, Thor's hammer. Thor was the thunder god, the most popular god among Viking warriors. "So, by naming your ship *Wind-weaver*, you honour Njord and hope that he'll keep the storms away and send the fish to you?" he asked respectfully.

"What? No, it's just a name, you idiot," said Orm. He glanced at Corvus' amulet, glaring at the younger man from under shaggy white eyebrows, a glint of humour in his rheumy eyes.

Realising Orm had been leading him on, Corvus made a face. In fact, for a fisherman, Orm cared surprisingly little about the gods and spirits. He seemed to positively enjoy ribbing those more superstitious than he. Corvus didn't like being made fun of, but Orm was a longtime friend of his family and an elder. Corvus owed him respect and obedience.

"I went to the market today," said Orm, changing the subject.

Corvus looked at him. He already knew that – Orm had left him behind to recaulk the clinker-built hull of his boat. It'd been hard, dirty work and had taken him all day, while Orm had been in town, selling fish and drinking ale, no doubt. Corvus waited for Orm to say more, but nothing was forthcoming.

"And?" said Corvus, somewhat irritated. Sometimes you had to drag the words out of Orm.

"There was talk," said Orm.

"Yes?" said Corvus, a little more irritated.

"Talk of Ullr's Ring."

Corvus raised an eyebrow. Ullr was the god of the feud, and was often invoked when a court was convened, with a jury, and a presiding 'law-sayer' to decide on guilt and innocence. The Ring was so called as the elders, the jury (which could be in the hundreds) and the law-sayer formed a ring around the accused and the defendant. That way the court or 'Ring' could be convened anywhere – all you needed were the right people.

Orm went on. "There's talk of a court case to be brought against you by Kelda. For the wounding of her grandson, little Wulfric," he said.

Corvus was stunned for a moment. "But he wounded me. Stabbed me in the leg. And I spared him!" he stuttered.

"Aye, but there's 'sparing' and 'sparing', isn't there? You may not have killed him, but if you've maimed him or cut him or taken an eye or some-thing – blood money will have to be paid at the least," said Orm.

Corvus' jaw dropped. "You think I'd... I didn't... it was a scratch. A tiny scratch!"

"Kelda is claiming a near-mortal wound," said Orm.

"Hah!" exploded Corvus. "It was a tiny splinter of wood that scratched his cheek! It barely drew blood, by Thor's arse!"

Orm looked Corvus up and down for a moment with an appraising look in his eye. Then he shrugged. "I believe you. But she's cunning, old Kelda. Cunning as a fox. Will they believe you in Ullr's Ring?"

Corvus frowned. It was so unfair. A wave of anger came over him. He was the wronged party here.

"But what about my family? My parents were *murdered* and my sisters carried off, just two weeks ago! My cause is just!" said Corvus.

"True enough, boy – but that's for a court to decide. But with you going to England, it'll look bad. They'll think you've fled because of guilt."

Corvus thought for a moment, but a moment only. There was nothing he could do about it. He couldn't stay here and fight a legal battle. He had to find his sisters before it was too late. Wulfric already had a head start on him.

"I must go to England," said Corvus resignedly.

"Well, without you there to tell your side of the story, they'll probably find against you," said Orm. "Outlaw you – at the very least demand a blood-price of gold. And compensation for the wooden doors to Wulfric's hall; they're saying you destroyed them completely."

"The doors as well! By Thor's hammer, is there no limit to the depths they will sink to? Pah, I'll never pay a penny to that murdering dog Wulfric, or his Hel-cursed family," spat Corvus bitterly.

"You could call a court of your own against Wulfric; get yourself a law-sayer. Make your case," Orm suggested.

"Bah! Not I," said Corvus dismissively. "I'll have his head, not his gold! Anyway, I have my sisters to think of."

Orm nodded. He'd expected as much. The youth of today – so hotheaded and swift to action. Especially this one. Still, it would be interesting. There might even be a saga in it.

"If you are outlawed, any Norseman can kill you on sight," Orm went on. "But you won't be around anyway. You might have to be careful when you come back, though. *If* you come back, of course," he added with a wry smile.

"Thanks – a comforting thought," said Corvus drily.

"You should have thought about it a bit more.

You should have come to me first, rather than just hacking your way into Wulfric's hall," said Orm.

Corvus sighed. "Aye, you're right. But I was so angry. I didn't stop to think."

Orm looked him over. Corvus looked like a war god. He was powerfully built, with eyes of steely blue, a born warrior like his father. But he was young, lacking in wisdom, rash and impulsive. For all his years away, he still had a lot to learn. His solution to any problem was a pair of axes. Still, where he was going, that might not be such a bad thing.

With that the conversation tailed off, and soon Nott, the goddess of the night, rode across the sky in her chariot of shadows, while Orm and Corvus slept.

When the god of the day, Dagr, son of Nott, returned, he brought bright sunshine, ideal weather for sailing. Under Orm's supervision, Corvus packed the boat with supplies – tools, rope, spare sail and other gear, plus a barrel of water and a barrel of salted fish. More's the pity, thought Corvus; he was already sick of fish. Fried fish, boiled fish, salted fish, fish broth and fish soup. It was all that Orm ever ate by the look of him, and all they were going to get for the next few days as well. Oh, for some roast lamb or beef!

Orm climbed into the boat and signalled to Corvus to push it out to sea. Corvus heaved and sweated, and after a moment or two of effort, the boat began to inch seaward. As it floated free, he leapt aboard, glancing at Orm in irritation. The old man had done nothing to help, leaving all the work to Corvus. But he couldn't complain too much. It was Orm's boat, after all, and he was doing Corvus a favour.

"Right, get that sail up," said Orm, "and take her out to sea." With that, he folded his arms, lay back against the prow and closed his eyes. That old dog, Corvus thought. Orm sleeps while I do all the work, eh? And was that the trace of a smile on the old man's lips? Corvus sighed. Raising the sail, he adjusted the ropes and sat down to man the rudder, sending the *Wind-weaver* scudding westward across the sea towards England.

"I don't like the look of that," Orm said suddenly

a few minutes later.

"What?" said Corvus. He'd been looking out to sea, judging the wind, and hadn't noticed that the old man wasn't asleep any more.

Orm pointed back to the shore, now a good distance away. Corvus could just make out what looked like an old woman on the beach. Her arms were raised to the skies, and she moved from foot to foot, as if acting out some strange ritual. Corvus squinted. It looked as if she had a pair of live snakes writhing around her arms. Before her was a small smoky fire – some kind of burnt offering to the gods, no doubt.

"By the sleet-cold halls of Hel, is that Kelda?" said Corvus.

"Aye, and it looks like she's laying a curse on us," said Orm.

Corvus blanched. A curse? How was that possible? Reflexively he reached for an axe, but caught himself. You couldn't split a curse in two with an axe.

"Should we go back – stop her?" he asked Orm.

"No, no – it's too late. She'd be long gone by

the time we got there," said Orm in a remarkably unconcerned manner.

"But a curse... we can't sail under a curse, surely?" said Corvus.

"Don't worry about it, boy," said Orm confidently.

"Have you got a warding or talisman against curses, then? A blessing of Njord or something?" said Corvus.

"Hah! No, of course not," said Orm, laughing. "She's just a crazy old hag who thinks she's a witch."

Corvus frowned. "How can you be so sure her curse won't harm us?" he said.

Orm shrugged, looking at Corvus with amusement in his eyes.

"You'll attack an armed stockade on your own, but at the sight of an old woman with a snake, you're quaking in your boots!" he said with a mocking smile.

That made Corvus angry. But he couldn't take it out on Orm, so he shook an angry fist at the dwindling figure on the beach. Curses and court cases – and it was *her* son who'd murdered Corvus' family and kidnapped his sisters! He should be cursing her.

She was a wily old bird; that was for sure, thought Corvus. Maybe he should have killed her, back there in Wulfric's hall. But where was the glory in that? The Valkyries, those daughters of Odin, the choosers of the slain, didn't take the souls of men to Valhalla for killing women and children. They took only heroes and great warriors.

Corvus sighed. He didn't share Orm's confidence about magic and curses. Then again, Orm had been around a lot longer than Corvus. He glanced over at him. The old man had gone back to his nap, mouth open, a thin sliver of drool crawling down his chin. Yes, he'd been around a *lot* longer.

As the *Wind-weaver* pulled away under a good wind, the shore and its evil dancing hag faded from sight. In spite of everything, Corvus couldn't help feeling excited. The land of his birth was behind him, perhaps forever. Who knew what adventures lay ahead, what new glories and challenges? The sun warmed his bones, the wind was full, the sharp tang of the sea filled his nostrils, and the white-topped waves sang the song of the whale road.

Corvus' heart soared, and he let all thoughts of curses and hag-witches fall behind him in the wake of the *Wind-weaver*.

CHAPTER 3

THE SEA DRAGON

They sailed for the rest of the day without incident or activity. For Orm, that is – Corvus had had to do pretty much everything that needed to be done, steering and watching the sails while Orm dozed or munched on fish or told tales of the gods.

When the goddess Nott brought night in her black chariot, the sea was calm and Corvus anchored the boat under Orm's nagging supervision. They slept peacefully on deck under a light breeze.

The next day dawned bright and clear and Corvus resumed his duties, sailing the *Windweaver* ever westward. If this weather held, they could expect to arrive at their destination by evening. They were looking for the Saxon shore – that part of England occupied by various Saxon kingdoms. Their destination was the land of the South Saxons, though if they were off course they would reach the land of the East Saxons or even the West Saxons.

After some time, Corvus spotted a sliver of earth on the horizon. He nudged Orm awake. Orm looked around, checked the position of the sun and examined the shoreline.

"England. South Saxons. We're on course. Look out for more land over there," he said, pointing in a southerly direction. With that, he turned over and went back to sleep. Corvus frowned in irritation. The old dog! Not even a word of praise for his seamanship.

More time passed, and as the sun moved across the sky, the Saxon shore drew ever closer. Soon Corvus could make out great white cliffs, looming skyward. Over on the left, more land appeared on the horizon, as Orm had said it would. The land of the Franks – they were still on course.

As Corvus sat at the rudder, glaring resentfully

at the dozing Orm, he noticed a dark cloud on the horizon to the east. Just then, Orm sat up, nose twitching.

"I smell storms," he said.

Orm certainly knew his stuff when it came to the sea, thought Corvus. "Aye," he replied, pointing east, "over there, behind us. But far away. I don't think it'll trouble us."

Orm stared at the dark smudge in the sky. He frowned. "It's coming this way, fast."

Corvus looked again. It *was* moving fast, like a black cloak being drawn across the sea.

"Strange. It's like nothing I've ever seen before," Orm said, his brow furrowed in puzzlement. That worried Corvus. Orm had spent nigh on fifty years as a sailor – surely he had seen everything by now?

The storm front swept in with unnatural speed. Orm was galvanised into action, shouting orders as he and Corvus stowed the gear, lashed things in place, took the sail down and generally prepared for a severe battering. Once that was done, they lashed themselves to the mast so they wouldn't be washed overboard by raging storm waves. A bitter wind swept over them, followed by bitingly cold rain that came in almost horizontally, stabbing their faces like arrowheads of ice. The heavens darkened, and a twilight gloom covered the sea. Thunder cracked the sky, and lightning split the darkness.

"Thor's hammer," muttered Orm.

"What?" shouted Corvus.

"Thunder. They say it is the sound of Thor's hammer as he does battle with the storm-giants. It is the sound of Ragnarök, the world's end!" shouted Orm over the raging tempest. Corvus fingered the amulet of Thor's hammer he wore around his neck.

A bolt of white-hot lightning suddenly struck the sea nearby, boiling it for an instant, giving off a blast of heat and steam. Another struck, even closer. Corvus and Orm looked at each other. Neither had seen anything like this before. It was unreal, unnatural.

With a thunderous crack, another bolt struck, this time on the other side, bathing both of them in hot, steaming seawater. Corvus thought it was almost as if Thor himself was trying to burst their little boat asunder with his hammer.

Corvus grasped again at his amulet. He began to mutter a prayer. A thought appeared in the back of his mind. Was this the work of that hag-witch, Kelda?

Another bolt struck, a few yards to their left. But if this was Thor, why did he keep missing the boat? He was a god, after all. And Kelda couldn't control a god, surely? In any case, it was almost as if the lightning was being aimed at the sea, not at their boat. Corvus looked over at Orm. Perhaps he'd know.

But Orm looked terrified. And that really, really worried Corvus.

Two more loud cracks followed in quick succession, as a pair of lightning bolts struck a patch of sea off to the starboard. The water steamed and boiled. Then it continued bubbling, though there was no more lightning. The storm seemed to be easing off now, fading as fast as it had come. The rain was beginning to ease, and the sky appeared brighter. But the bolt-struck waters still roiled and boiled. Great bubbles rose up and burst into the air, releasing a foul stench of rot, like the breath of a hundred drowned sailors. The clouds parted a little, and in the growing light Corvus could see something dark and indistinct rising up out of the depths.

Suddenly, a huge serpentine head broke the surface of the sea, great gouts of water cascading down its scaly, ridged skull and its sinuous, heavily muscled neck. A hulking body, scaled, greenish, pitted with barnacles, finned and tailed like a demon-whale, came up behind. It raised its head and uttered a low, rumbling roar that shook Corvus and Orm to their very bones. Its eyes were black and soulless, wet and cruel, and they glittered with evil. A foul, sea-rot stink filled the air.

"Aieee!" shrieked Orm at the top of his voice, "Jormungand, it is Jormungand!"

Jormungand! thought Corvus. Jormungand was the world serpent, the gigantic worm that eats its own tail and would kill Thor himself at Ragnarök, the last battle of the gods at the end of time. They were doomed!

Corvus looked at the great beast as its head reared up over the small boat. Well, if he was going to die, he would go to Valhalla fighting with the last drop of his blood. Quickly Corvus plucked the long knife from his belt and began to saw at the rope that held him to the mast. If only they'd realised the true nature of the threat, instead of lashing themselves down, they should have been... what? What could they do against this thing? He glanced over at Orm. The old man was desperately working at his own bonds, his eyes staring in unbelieving terror at the sea serpent.

As Corvus broke free, the scaled, diamond-shaped head of the sea dragon flashed down, its great maw gaping, rows of sharp sword-teeth glistening in the sun. Its jaws closed around Orm and the mast, snapping the wood like a matchstick. Orm shrieked in agony as the serpent took him into the air. His chest burst asunder, spraying blood and entrails, soaking Corvus in gore. Orm's head fell one way, his legs another. Hungrily, greedily, the vile beast gulped down the rest of him as Corvus scrabbled for his axes.

Orm had died a ghastly death, right in front of his eyes! Corvus felt a twinge of guilt – all Orm had been trying to do was give Corvus a helping hand, and now he was dead.

As the beast fed, plucking the remaining pieces of Orm's body from the sea, blood dribbling down the sides of its cavernous mouth, Corvus' mind raced. The world serpent was supposed to be huge, a beast that did battle with the gods. Certainly this thing was big, but it actually wasn't more than twenty feet from mouth to tail. Well, maybe thirty. It just wasn't big enough to be Jormungand. Maybe it wasn't some mythological creature from the land of the gods. Maybe it was just some ancient predator of the depths. And if it was just a beast, it could be killed. Corvus' heart filled with hope and with white-hot rage. He would avenge Orm! He would kill this foul beast of the sea!

Just then, the sea serpent's head came crashing down again, jaws agape, breath like a cesspool of the deep. Corvus leapt aside, narrowly avoiding the sea dragon's head, which smashed into the prow of the boat, shattering it. As the serpent reared back up, ready for another strike, Corvus hurled an axe with all his might, straight at its head. The axe struck true, but it glanced off the creature's tough, bony scales like an arrow on a full steel helm. Corvus was flummoxed. The sea serpent's skin was like chain mail. And now he was down to one axe.

Corvus roared in rage, screaming his battle cry to the skies. He stood, covered in Orm's blood and entrails, axe in one hand, long knife in the other, yelling his defiance as the gigantic sea serpent readied its head for another strike. Behind him, dark clouds roiled and thunder boomed. Did the beast pause briefly, unsure? Was it intimidated by this strange man-thing that showed no fear? Perhaps, but not for long, for it thrashed down once more, jaws biting. Corvus waited until the last second, then stepped aside, bringing his axe down with all his great strength on the beast's neck, just as its head smashed on to the deck. Corvus' axe split one of the bony scales apart, but it could not bite deep and drew no blood.

With the serpent's last, shattering blow, the boat began to break apart. Water was rushing in. Soon it would sink, and Corvus would be almost defence-less in the water. He had to try something else.

As the head came down for its fourth strike, Corvus stood, waiting. The boat was taking on water, and already his feet were submerged. This might be his only chance. He swung his axe, aiming for the side of the head. With a bit of luck he might take out an eye, though bony ridges protected it above and below the socket. His aim was slightly off, but it was a blow so powerful that it knocked the sea serpent's head to the side, halting its downward trajectory. It hung in the air for a moment, stunned.

Nimbly, Corvus dropped his axe and leapt up on to the creature's neck, securing a handhold under one of its scales, long dagger at the ready. The sea serpent whipped up its head, trying to shake Corvus free. Grimly he held on, working his long knife in between two of its scales and driving it deep. Black blood, thick like treacle, began to ooze around the knife, but the sea serpent appeared not to notice. Again it swung its head rapidly from side to side, twisting, trying to shake him free.

Corvus forced the knife in to the hilt. No effect. He tried another spot. Nothing. The serpent struck furiously at the remains of the boat, splitting it in two, and the *Wind-weaver* sank beneath the waves, leaving only splintered wood and the remains of its mast floating on the surface. If Corvus fell into the water, he was doomed.

He had to kill this thing. He began to inch his way forwards on its neck, clinging with all his strength. The beast whipped its head from side to side, shaking him to the bone, but he held on.

After a moment or two, he'd managed to crawl into a position just behind the sea serpent's head. Raising his long dagger, he plunged it deep into one of the creature's eyes. The beast shrieked in pain, a sound like steel on stone, magnified a hundred times. Corvus stabbed again. The sea dragon writhed in agony, shaking its head more vigorously then ever. But Corvus held on and stabbed once more. Fluid burst out of the wreck of its eye, and the beast shrieked again. Then it plunged downwards, trying to escape the sharp, stinging thing on its back and return to the safety of the deep.

As the sea serpent struck the water with a mighty splash, Corvus took a deep breath. He wasn't going to let this thing live, not after it had killed Orm, even if it cost him his own life. They began to plummet into the salty depths. Something round and hard knocked against Corvus' leg, and he glanced down. With a shudder of revulsion, he recognised Orm's head, eyes open, seeming to stare at Corvus in silent outrage at his hideous fate. The head fell away, and sank into the endless dark below.

Galvanised by horror and rage, Corvus plunged his knife to the hilt into the beast's other eye. The sea serpent gave out a low, booming moan. Corvus responded by stabbing deeper, seeking out the brain, driving the knife further into the creature's eye socket. Suddenly, the sea serpent stiffened and went limp. Corvus realised he must have penetrated the brain at last. Letting go, he swam up to the light, as fast as he could, his lungs aching. Below him, the great sea dragon slowly spiralled downwards to join Orm's head in the yawning blackness of the deep.

Corvus burst forth into the light, and drew in a great shuddering breath. He'd made it! But he was alone in the middle of the sea. He looked around and spotted the *Wind-weaver*'s mast, floating on the waves. He swam over and grabbed it. There was still some rope wrapped around it, so he lashed himself on to the shaft. The storm had passed away as if it had never been, and the sea was calm, the sun shining. He could see the shores of England in the distance. He kicked, swimming landward, thinking about what had just happened. Could Kelda really have used some kind of dark magic against him? Had she used the storm to summon the sea dragon? His heart felt heavy as he thought about his old friend. Still, what was done was done. The Three Goddesses, the Norns, weavers of man's destiny, had decided Orm's fate long ago, and there was little Corvus could do about it.

He kept swimming shoreward as long as he could, inching his way towards land, but as darkness fell, hunger, thirst and exhaustion overtook him, and he drifted into unconsciousness. If he hadn't tied himself to the mast, he would have slipped under the surface to join Orm in his watery grave.

CHAPTER 4

THE SAXON SHORE

*C*orvus groaned. Memories of his mother, raven-haired and dark-eyed, and his father, blue-eyed and blond, the picture of a Viking, had been smiling down at him in a dream. But something was wrong. Blood and anger, fire and treachery crouched, ready to pounce, at his parents' shoulders, before the dream images faded from his waking mind.

A terrible thirst racked his body. He tried opening his eyes, but his lids were stuck together. He reached up a hand and weakly cleared away the salty grunge that mired his vision. Eyes stinging, he looked around.

He was washed up on a pebbly beach, still lashed to the splintered mast of the *Wind-weaver*. He had nothing save the amulet of Thor's hammer around his neck and the tattered remains of his clothes. His leather boots were long gone; he had no food, water or weapons. His chain mail jerkin, money, axes and everything else had joined Orm in the land below the waves. But he was still alive. Weak, exhausted, but alive. He'd made it!

The sea was lapping at his feet, and he realised the tide was coming in. He'd better get further inland or he'd drown. Managing to untie himself from the mast, he began to crawl up the beach. Eventually, he made it beyond the tide line, but even that simple effort exhausted him and he fell into a deep sleep.

♦♦♦♦♦♦

Corvus was rudely awoken by a dull pain in his side. Someone was kicking him in the ribs.

"What have we here?" said a voice.

Judging by the accent it was a Saxon voice, thought Corvus as he looked up, blinking in the harsh glare of the midday sun. There were two people standing over him. The one who'd kicked him was a young woman, tall and skinny, in hunter's leathers, a bow over her shoulder and a single-edged long knife, or scramseax as the Saxons called them, at her belt. She was gaunt-faced with hollow cheeks, dark brown eyes and long brown hair tied behind. Thin, but not bad-looking, Corvus thought to himself. The other was a man, much older, grey-haired, grizzled and weather-beaten, with a net draped over his shoulder and a fish knife hanging on his belt. Father and daughter perhaps. The man reminded him of Orm, and a wave of sorrow came over him.

"What's your name, boy?" said the man.

Corvus squinted up at the Saxon. He tried to speak but found himself barely able to croak through his dry, cracked lips, "Water..."

The young woman looked at her companion. The old man nodded, and the woman knelt down beside Corvus, dribbling water into his mouth from a water skin. Reflexively, Corvus grabbed for the skin and began gulping.

"Steady, now. Take it easy," said the woman,

pulling the skin from his greedy lips. She was right. Too much water when you were this parched could do more harm than good. But the few gulps Corvus had taken had an almost immediate effect. He began to feel better, strength returning to his exhausted limbs. Coughing and heaving, he pulled himself up into a sitting position. Warily, the two Saxons stepped back, hands on their dagger hilts. Corvus was a big man, heavily muscled and lithe, and despite his weakened state, still an intimidating figure.

"What's your name?" asked the man again.

"Corvus. Corvus Gunnarson," said Corvus without thinking.

The Saxons both frowned. "Gunnarson. That's a Viking name, isn't it?" said the man.

"Aye, what of it?" said Corvus, a flash of pride and defiance in his steely blue eyes.

"We've had a lot of trouble with Vikings. Bloody killers – burning, pillaging," said the young woman, fingering her knife.

"Don't worry about me – I'm not that kind of Viking," said Corvus.

"Well, you would say that, wouldn't you?" said the woman, eyeing Corvus with suspicion.

Corvus had to admit she had a point. He was hardly going to tell them he was a ruthless marauding raider, and the best thing they could do to protect their homes and families was to kill him immediately!

"True enough," he said, and shrugged. There was a moment of silence as each looked the other over. Corvus noticed a cross hanging around the man's neck. That meant he was a Christian. Many Saxons were still pagans, but more were converting to the White Christ every year, as were many Danes and other Vikings, in fact.

"Corvus – that's a strange name for a Viking," said the man eventually.

"Aye, it's Latin. My mother was a follower of the White Christ. From the southlands." Corvus had learnt a bit of the language of Christian worship from his mother, and had picked up a smattering of Saxon and other languages during his years in service to the Danish king. In any case, the Norse and Saxon languages were very similar.

"You're not a Christian yourself, though, are you?" said the man, pointing at Corvus' amulet.

"No, my father followed the old ways, as do I. And Corvus means raven. We hold the raven in high esteem, so it's a good Viking name, even if it is in Latin. And then there's my hair," said Corvus, fingering his shaggy locks, salt-stained but still as black as the raven.

Things seemed to have reached an impasse.

A huge warrior, athletic and powerfully built, had just washed up on the Saxon fisherman's beach. His eyes were a bright, steely blue, with a blazing wildness about them, and it turned out he was a Viking. Problem.

Normally, Corvus could have taken these two out, even though he was unarmed, but he was weak, alone in a foreign land, and in any case, he had no desire to kill a couple of fisherfolk. There was no glory in that. Not to mention the fact that they could have killed him as he lay on the beach – instead they had given him water. Though if they'd known he was a Viking in the first place, perhaps they would have killed him.

Corvus tried to defuse things by adding, "I respect the Church of the White Christ. My mother was a good woman. I have nothing against them, unlike some of my Norse kin."

The man nodded. He seemed to believe Corvus. "I'm Hengist," he said. "This is my daughter, Merewyn."

"Greetings to you both. Where am I, anyway?" asked Corvus.

"Sussex. Our village, Wotanhirst, is nearby," said Hengist.

"Sussex? Where's that?" said Corvus.

"The kingdom of the South Saxons," said Merewyn.

Well, at least he'd arrived in the right part of the world, Corvus thought. Hengist leant forward and offered a hand. Corvus took it, and Hengist heaved him to his feet. Corvus swayed for a moment. He felt weak and dizzy.

"You'll have to come back to Wotanhirst with us," said Hengist.

"And what if I don't want to?" said Corvus.

They looked at each other. The man took the net

from his shoulder, and the young woman reached for her knife. Corvus drew himself up to his full height and stood back, fists at the ready. He towered above them, muscles rippling, and gave them his most warlike scowl. Hengist and Merewyn stepped back involuntarily, fear on their faces. The young woman audibly gulped.

But the effort made Corvus stagger. The Saxons exchanged looks, and the man made a wry face. Corvus was weakened, but they really didn't want to tangle with him, even in the state he was in. He still looked formidable.

"You need food and water," Hengist said. "You won't survive long out here on your own."

"I'll get by. Just leave me be, and we can all walk away from this," said Corvus. He felt sick, and his knees were about to give out, but he wouldn't let them know how bad a state he was in. He could still bluff his way out of this.

The Saxons seemed to be thinking for a moment, then Hengist sighed. "We can't just let you wander about on your own. You're a Viking, after all. I think you're honest enough, but how can we know for sure?"

Corvus flicked his fringe of black hair away from his eyes and nodded. He could see their point. The Vikings had a very bad reputation among the Saxons of England, and with good reason. Which was why he didn't like the idea of going back to their village. On the other hand, they might know something about Wulfric.

"And what will be my fate if I go with you?" Corvus asked.

"Cearl, the village chieftain, will decide," said Merewyn.

"And what if he decides to have me killed?" said Corvus.

"That's a risk you'll have to take. Though it's more likely he'll make a slave of you," said Hengist.

"A slave! Hah! You will have to kill me before I become one of them!" said Corvus angrily.

"Aye, I figured that from the look of you," said Hengist, "and what use is a dead slave, eh?" He grinned. Corvus smiled grimly back.

Hengist went on, "On the other hand, the chief's

a reasonable man. Perhaps you can convince him to let you go on your way."

Corvus raised an eyebrow. That didn't sound like a good bet. He decided to try another tack.

"Have you heard of a Viking called Wulfric Cold-blood?" he asked.

The reaction was instant: Their faces took on a stony look, and their eyes narrowed. Hengist grimaced, and Merewyn spat on the ground. This was what Corvus had been hoping for. If he could establish a common enemy, maybe he could win their trust.

"Wulfric Cold-blood and his war band, the Slaughter Wolves, that band of murdering thugs? Aye, we have. What do you want with him? Are you one of his men?" Hengist said, hand resting once more on the hilt of his dagger.

"By Odin's fury, no! I have sworn a Blood Oath to take his head!" said Corvus passionately.

"I don't believe it! Why?" said Merewyn.

"He murdered my parents, and took my sisters – the stinking dog!" said Corvus. He tried to spit on the ground as well, but his mouth was so dry nothing came out, making him feel rather foolish – he couldn't even spit. Merewyn put her hand over her mouth, stifling a nervous giggle. Corvus scowled at her.

"Well," said Hengist, "that's a surprise. As it happens, Wulfric has bought some land from Oslac, the king of Sussex. He says he wants to settle peacefully and establish trade. But he's also built himself a fort and populated it with warriors, not farmers. Now why would he do that, if he was intending to settle down, all peaceful like? And stuff keeps going missing – a sheep here, a horse there. I say he's just bought that doddering fool Oslac off with gold while he builds up his strength. It won't be long before he goes on the attack, I reckon."

"Pah! Vikings! They're all the same – blood-thirsty, murdering scum, the lot of them!" spat Merewyn.

Corvus glared at her. "Er, present company excepted, of course," Merewyn said hurriedly.

"Well," said Hengist. "It appears we have a common enemy. This will go down well with Cearl, who has no love for Wulfric. Will you come with us now? I shall put in a good word for you, and Cearl will listen to me."

Having heard this, Corvus he felt a lot better about going with Hengist. With luck, he could trade labour for food, armour and weapons. Also, the chances were that Cearl would know where Wulfric's settlement was.

Corvus relaxed, and smiled. "Aye, Hengist, I'll go with you." Hengist smiled back. A relieved-looking Merewyn handed Corvus her water skin and a small cloth bundle of food.

"Here, eat, drink. Get some of your strength back – it's a good half-hour walk back to Wotan-hirst," said Merewyn.

Corvus grinned. "My thanks," he said, clapping Merewyn on the shoulder in a polite gesture of friendship. He didn't see her grimacing in pain from the force of the slap nor glare at him in annoyance – the water skin took all his attention.

He drank off a gulp or two, careful not to take too much, and then turned his attention to the cloth bundle. He was ravenous! He opened it up, ready to eat the lot in a couple of mouthfuls. His heart sank. It was fish. Salted fish…

CHAPTER 5

SLAUGHTER WOLVES

Wotanhirst was a typical Saxon village, well sited for defence. Corvus thought it seemed peaceful, resting atop a wooded hill with a stream that ran down into the valley below. Wotanhirst actually meant 'Wotan's Hill', Wotan being the Saxon chief god, their version of Odin, king of the Norse gods. Enclosed by a simple wooden stockade, the village also had a wooden gate with a tall watchtower above it. Rectangular houses of wattle and daub, with thatched roofs and gently smoking chimney holes, were scattered around a central market square. A larger, more elaborate wooden hall stood prominently on the edge – the chief, Cearl's, hall. There was also a new wooden church devoted to the White Christ. All in all, it was quite a small village, with about 150 inhabitants.

Hengist led Corvus straight to Cearl. Corvus had drawn stares from the villagers on the way in, but with Hengist and Merewyn beside him, people didn't seem that concerned. Cearl turned out to be a burly man in his late thirties, with a barrel chest, a pot belly of prodigious girth, a great mane of blond hair and a big blond Saxon beard that flowed down his chest like a river of gold. He was suspicious of Corvus at first, but softened after hearing him curse Wulfric. When Hengist agreed to take responsibility (and liability!) for Corvus, he agreed to let him stay in the village, working off the cost of his food and lodging by doing odd jobs. So it was that an exhausted Corvus found himself a place to stay at Hengist's house. He passed out almost immediately after supper and slept until dawn, a deep sleep of exhaustion.

The next morning, Corvus sat with Hengist in his hut, wolfing down stew – potatoes, vegetables and lamb, leftovers from the night before and a welcome change from fish. Outside, they heard a sudden shout. The noise spread until it seemed the whole village was in an uproar of alarm.

Hengist ran outside. Cursing his luck, Corvus put down the bowl of delicious stew (if only every breakfast could be a meat stew!) and ran after him, hoping he'd get the chance to come back and finish his meal.

Outside, all was bedlam. The guard on the watchtower by the main gate was shouting. People, dogs and even pigs were running about as if at random. Mothers were snatching up their children, and men were arming themselves as fast as they could.

Corvus spotted Cearl outside his hall, bellowing orders, while his two children belted a mail shirt over his massive frame. In one hand he held a full-face Saxon helm, in the other a long two-handed battleaxe. Near him the blacksmith had already begun to hand out weapons to the men of fighting age.

Corvus ran towards the watchtower.

"Vikings, Vikings!" the sentry was shouting, pointing down the hill to the valley. "Armed and visored for battle, coming this way!"

Down below, marching uphill towards them, was a large band of Viking warriors. Shielding his eyes from the sun, Corvus could just make out the standard that fluttered in the wind at the front. It was red, with a grey figure of some kind. As he tried to make it out, Hengist came up beside him, a leather cuirass on his chest, a shield on one arm and a spear in the other.

"Who are they?" he asked Corvus, "Do you know them?"

Corvus shook his head. "Can't tell yet," he said, flicking strands of raven hair out of his eyes. Then he gasped in surprise. "The she-wolf!" he blurted out.

"The what?" said Hengist.

Corvus turned to Hengist. "It's the battle banner of the Slaughter Wolves, the she-wolf at bay. It is the flag of Wulfric Cold-blood himself!"

Hengist scowled and spat. "I knew he would come. He has taken us by surprise! And our accursed king let him in – how easily he was fooled."

But Corvus was thinking of other things. If the battle banner was there, that meant Wulfric was there as well. And if there was to be a battle, maybe he'd get the chance to kill Wulfric.

Corvus turned to Hengist. "Give me a weapon and some armour, and I'll fight with you. I'll try and get to Wulfric and kill him!" he said.

Hengist didn't reply. His face had gone pale at the sight of the approaching band. "There must be two hundred, maybe two hundred and fifty of them. We have only thirty warriors, half of those unblooded striplings."

Corvus frowned. Hengist was right. Corvus also realised he couldn't just kill Wulfric outright either. He had to find out where his sisters were first. This was going to be difficult.

"Come on!" the older man yelled, running back into the village. Corvus followed, hot on his heels. Hengist dashed up to Cearl and told him the bad news.

Cearl cursed. "We can't fight that many. We'll have to see if we can pay them off," he said, his voice a deep, throaty growl. "But the price will be high." He looked over at Corvus. "And what about you, Viking? What will you do?"

Corvus drew himself up to his full height, his blue eyes glinting. "Give me an axe, and any armour you can spare. I will stand and fight by your side and die with you if it comes to that," he said.

Cearl stared at him for a moment, judging the truth of his words. Then he nodded, seemingly satisfied. "Your courage does you credit, Viking warrior," he said, offering Corvus one of his own axes.

Next, the chieftain called over his young son, who by the look of him had not seen thirteen summers. Corvus heard him telling the boy to ride with all haste to Selsea, capital city of the South Saxons, and tell King Oslac that Wulfric was on the rampage. "Tell him to bring his army, and don't let the Vikings catch you!" he shouted as the lad sped away.

Then Cearl strode off to the gate, assuming that Wulfric would send a herald first to negotiate, as that was usually the way with these things. They'd have to buy the Vikings off with what they called Danegeld – probably most, if not all, of their wealth – but with luck they could avoid bloodshed. As he passed Corvus, he said, "Come with me, Corvus. You are the most experienced warrior we have here, even if you are a Norseman. I will need your advice."

Corvus nodded, though his heart sank. If he was their most experienced warrior, they were in trouble. Sure, he'd fought for the Danish king in a battle and several skirmishes, but he was hardly a seasoned veteran! Still, Corvus was impressed by Cearl. The bulky chief was a no-nonsense warrior, decisive and a good leader. He would be a fair captain if there was to be a battle.

While the Vikings were approaching, Corvus got hold of some patchy pieces of leather armour and a shield. He had to sling the shield on his back, because you couldn't carry a shield while using the weapon Cearl had given him – a huge two-handed Danish battleaxe. Corvus would have preferred a pair of large hand-axes, but he'd been trained to use the two-handed battleaxe while in service to the king of the Danes. It was capable of smashing shields and helmets, and in the hands of a powerful warrior, it could split a man clean in two, though you needed some space to wield it properly. When he was ready, Corvus hurried after Cearl. Hengist and Merewyn fell in beside him; he noticed that the young woman was armed with a bow, hunter's leathers and her scramseax at her belt.

They passed a row of warriors, waiting to be blessed by the village priest, who walked down the line making the sign of the cross and marking their foreheads with holy water. Corvus frowned. Cearl was right; many of them were no more than lads. They were a poorly equipped bunch, with spears and shields but little or no armour, save for leather caps. Cearl had the only mail shirt in the village. Corvus saw that apart from Merewyn, the women and young children had retreated to the huts at the centre of the village.

Wulfric and his war band were drawing closer, as Corvus came up beside Cearl at the gates.

"Will he talk?" asked Cearl.

Corvus shook his head. "I doubt it. He doesn't

really need to. They don't call him Cold-blood for nothing. He's ruthless, greedy and murderous."

The approaching war band – the Slaughter Wolves of Wulfric Cold-blood – came to a halt, the men drawing up in formation. Many of them wore wolf-head skins or wolf skulls over their helmets. Corvus could see that Hengist's original estimate of 200 or 250 was accurate. Then a small group of about ten lightly armoured men walked on ahead, approaching the village.

"Ah, it looks like you're wrong, Corvus. They want to parley after all. Maybe we can get out of this with our heads intact, eh?" Cearl said optimistically.

"Be careful, Cearl. Something doesn't feel right. You can't trust a man like Wulfric," said Corvus.

As if to underscore Corvus' words, the Viking advance party broke into a sudden dash for the gates. Behind them, the war band gave a great shout of "Slaughter, slaughter!" – Wulfric's war cry – and began to charge up the hill. If the advance party managed to keep the gates open long enough for the main body to get there, the village would be overwhelmed in seconds!

"They're trying to rush the gates! Get back inside and shut them, fast!" bellowed Cearl.

"Hold on!" said Corvus, stepping forward.

"What are you doing?" said Cearl, reaching for his axe. "Is this treachery?"

"No, trust me – leave enough room for me to get back in!" said Corvus, stepping through the gate.

There was little time to say more, as the first of the Viking runners was upon him. As the warrior closed in, he threw his spear at Corvus. Corvus batted it to the side with a push of his axe shaft, and then dropped to one knee, swinging his two-handed battleaxe in a great sweep. It carved through both the Viking's legs just below the knee. The man screamed and collapsed, dying in the mud.

Close behind him came another warrior, swinging his sword. Corvus wheeled, taking the blow on the shield slung on his back. He continued turning, bringing his axe round in an arc and chopping off the Viking's head, just like that. The head bounced back down the hill towards the onrushing

Slaughter Wolves, the helmet flying one way, the head flying another.

Two more Vikings came in, shields up, one thrusting his spear at Corvus' face, the other readying his axe. Corvus dodged the spear thrust, and aimed a massive overhead blow at the axe wielder, who put up his shield. Corvus' mighty blow shattered the shield as if it was pottery and carried on through, slicing his arm in two.

The man yelled in agony, dropped his axe and staggered back. His severed hand fell into the mud, still holding what was left of the shield. The other warrior thrust again with the spear. Corvus parried it with the shaft of his axe, and then smashed the blunt part of the axe-head into the spearman's face. The force of the blow burst his helmet apart and he fell backward, laid out on the ground, poleaxed. He was the lucky one – he might wake up with only a broken nose. At the same moment, four more of the advance guard rushed in. This was going to be hard, thought Corvus.

Just then, one of the men went down with a cry of pain, an arrow in his thigh. Merewyn had taken up a position in the watchtower, and was firing her bow down at them! Corvus gave a great roar, and charged forward while they were distracted, looking up at Merewyn. At the last minute, he dived into a forward roll, holding his axe in front of him with both hands. The shaft of his axe caught all three of them on their shins, bowling them over. Corvus was on his feet in an instant. He brought his axe down on the first, splitting the helmet and the skull beneath. The second was back on his feet – Corvus smashed him in the gut with the reverse end of his axe. The warrior staggered back, doubled over, only to receive an arrow from Merewyn straight through the back of the neck. He fell dead before he could take another breath. The third Viking was up and running for his life, back to the main body of the Vikings. The attempt to rush the gate had been foiled. Behind Corvus a great cheer went up.

But the rest of the Vikings – some 200 of them – gave a roar of rage, and came on fast. Corvus stepped nimbly back through the gate, and the Saxons closed it quickly, barring it with a heavy oak timber.

Corvus was met by much back-slapping and cheers. Many fists punched the air.

"Incredible!" shouted Cearl. "You're the best fighter I've ever seen!"

Corvus stood back from the celebration. The defeat of the advance guard was good for morale, but it was only the opening skirmish. Merewyn was looking down, obviously a little annoyed. It was clear she wasn't happy with Corvus getting all the credit – he'd be dead if it hadn't been for her. But there was no time to dwell on that, for they could hear the roar of the Vikings outside. The rest of Wulfric's force was on the way, and they only had a flimsy wooden stockade to keep them out. Suddenly there was a loud booming sound, and the gate shuddered.

Merewyn, still on the watchtower, shouted, "They've got a battering ram!" She fired down into them. There was a cry, but the ram – a great log – struck again. Then a volley of arrows flew up out of the main body of the Vikings towards Merewyn. She ducked behind the wooden wall of the tower only just in time. Luckily she wasn't hit, though a dozen arrows peppered the tower all around her, pinning her down. If she stood up she would be dead. There was another great crash at the gates. The oaken timber that barred the gate splintered slightly. It wouldn't be long before the Slaughter Wolves were through.

"Form a shield wall across the entrance!" bellowed Cearl.

Cearl, Corvus and Hengist stood behind the gate, the twenty-five or so other Saxon warriors fanning out to either side. They formed a shield wall, an arc of shields bristling with spears, around the gate. Corvus knew it was a last, desperate defence; there simply weren't enough of them. They might hold Wulfric's men back for a while, but once Wulfric's men were through the gate, it was just a matter of time before they were overcome by the sheer weight of numbers. He readied himself for Valhalla.

CHAPTER 6

ENEMY AT THE GATES

The wooden gates shuddered and shook. Splinters flew from the battered timbers. The next booming strike was followed by an ominous cracking sound, and the gate began to sag on its hinges.

Corvus looked to his left. Hengist's teeth were bared in desperate anger. On his right, Cearl spat and muttered a curse under his breath. A bead of sweat rolled down his face into his golden beard. Corvus hefted his axe and glared at the gate. In a few seconds the enemy would break through, and then there would be blood.

Suddenly the gate flew open with a thunderous

crack. There was a great shout of triumph, and several Viking warriors, wolf-head skins over iron helms, burst into the village, howling like madmen. They ran straight into the Saxon shield wall. Axes bit down and spears lashed out, and in moments most of the first rush of Viking warriors were cut down or reeling back, badly wounded.

Not a single Saxon had been scratched. The villagers grinned and shouted at this first victory. Corvus frowned. He knew about battles like this. It was never this easy. Cearl knew this too. The big chief spoke.

"Steady, lads, let's not get carried away. They weren't expecting us to be that organised. They'll be coming on for real now, so we'd better be ready for it."

Sure enough, a flurry of orders could be heard from beyond the shattered gate, and a few seconds later came the tramp of steady feet. A voice rose above the din, a bellowing voice resonant with malice, the voice of Wulfric Cold-blood.

"Call yourself Slaughter Wolves? These girlie vegetable-eaters shouldn't be giving you this much

trouble! Cut them down, cut them all down!"
shrieked the voice.

Corvus shivered. He had never met the man,
but this was the warrior who had killed his parents,
burnt his home and sold his sisters into slavery.
Rage rose up in him as he waited for the enemy's
next move.

The Vikings marched in through the gate, this
time in a wedge formation bristling with spears.
A large, heavily armoured warrior marched at the
apex of the wedge, his shield slung on his back and
a great axe in his fists. He was the wall-breaker. He
was flanked by shield men who would protect him
while he cut through the Saxon shield wall.

But the Vikings hadn't counted on Corvus being
there. Already he had sized up the wall-breaker,
judging his likely avenue of attack and searching
out his weak spots. Corvus let the shaft of his
own great axe fall through his hand until he was
gripping the head almost like a dagger. As the
champion strode forward, his axe sweeping down
in an overhead arc, Corvus stepped smartly in
under his strike, and drove his shield up hard

against his opponent's exposed wrist, breaking the man's grip on his axe. Then Corvus dropped to one knee, bringing his shield down sharply on his opponent's left foot and using the razored axe blade like a dagger to gouge a deep cut into the man's right foot. The champion bellowed in pain, his momentum carrying him forward over Corvus, just as Corvus had expected it would. Corvus straightened up, pitching him over his back, to slam on to the ground with a crash, where he was finished off by a Saxon. So much for their wall-breaker.

A groan of angry despair rose from the Viking shield wedge at the sight of their champion, so easily dispatched, but they came on anyway, grinding into the Saxon line, shield to shield. They heaved and shoved, but the thin Saxon line held. The Vikings couldn't get enough men through the narrow gate, so they were unable to bring the weight of their greater numbers to bear.

Corvus stepped back. Cearl and Hengist cursed him – they needed him in the line. They were straining to hold back the onrush of Vikings, Hengist jabbing with his spear and Cearl thrusting round his shield with his sword, his great axe slung on his back. Between them they had to close the gap Corvus had left. But not for long. Corvus slung his own shield and hefted his axe in both hands.

He stepped back a few more paces, noticing Cearl had one leg back, braced against the earth, straining to hold the enemy in place.

Corvus grinned. "Blood and battle!" he cried, sprinting forward. Cearl gave a grunt of surprise as Corvus ran up his leg and on to his back, then somersaulted into the air over the Saxon shield wall and into the midst of the Viking wedge! As he landed, he brought his axe down with such force that it split a Slaughter Wolf in two from the top of his helmet down to his breastbone. Blood fountained into the air. A moment later, Corvus was in the middle of the Viking line, laying about him with great blows of his axe, crushing skulls and limbs like paper. Within seconds, he'd cleared the front rank, and the Saxons surged forward, driving the Vikings back to the gate. Merewyn began shooting arrows from the tower into their backs, and suddenly the Viking wedge broke and ran, leaving behind at least fifteen dead and dying. For only two Saxon dead.

"How's that for girlie vegetable-eaters?" shouted Cearl at the top of his voice after the fleeing Vikings. The Saxons burst out laughing. Maybe they could actually win this after all.

But then Corvus noticed several large iron grappling hooks, flung over the tops of the wooden walls on either side of the gate. Cearl and Hengist had seen them, too, and their faces went pale, realising the Viking wedge had only been a diversion.

A chant began on the other side of the wall. "One, two, HEAVE! One, two, HEAVE!"

At each "HEAVE!" a hundred Vikings bellowed and pulled at the grappling hooks, wrenching at the walls, pulling them down. Already they were teetering backwards, the wood splintering and cracking. With the walls down, the Vikings could outflank the Saxon line with ease, overwhelming them in moments.

"Shield fort! Form a shield fort!" yelled Cearl at the top of his voice. "Now!"

The shield fort, or *skjaldborg* as it was called

by the Vikings, was a circle of interlocked shields, bristling with spears and axes. It was usually a last stand, a final desperate defence.

Corvus helped Cearl get the men together. Hengist called his daughter down and into the circle – she could fire her bow out from the centre of the armoured ring. They joined up, shield-to-shield, just in time. The walls came crashing down, and with a great angry roar the Vikings rushed in, surrounding the Saxons in seconds. They would not last long.

CHAPTER 7

WULFRIC COLD-BLOOD

Wulfric's Slaughter Wolves fell on the shield fort like a wave on the shore, probing, stabbing, slashing. The Saxons held at first, but slowly men began to fall, each death weakening the shield fort further.

Corvus struck hard and fought as he'd never fought before. All those who came against him died quickly, and the patch of earth in front of him turned red with gore. Soon Corvus found himself without an opponent – none would come against him.

Beside him, Hengist went down, a spear in his belly. He fell to the ground, his lifeblood emptying into the dirt. Corvus stepped over him to cover the space he had left.

"Father, Father!" cried Merewyn. Hengist coughed. Blood gushed from his mouth and Merewyn moaned in despair.

Hengist ignored his daughter. He gripped Corvus' arm, and through gritted teeth said, "Protect my daughter, Corvus, protect my daughter." His voice gurgled horribly as his throat filled with blood.

Corvus looked around. Wulfric's men were everywhere, and in any case he didn't think he was going to live long enough himself to protect Merewyn. But he owed a debt to Hengist, who could have left Corvus dying on the Saxon shore. Instead he had given him water, food and shelter.

"I will do my best," was all Corvus could say.

"Swear it!" gurgled Hengist.

"What?" said Corvus. "Swear it? We're all about to be..."

"SWEAR IT!"

Corvus gave in. "I swear it by Odin and Thor!" he said.

"Swear by the White Christ," said Hengist weakly.

"By the halls of Hel! All right, man, I swear it by the White Christ, too," said Corvus, as he parried a spear thrust and countered with whiplike speed, shattering his attacker's shield and sending him sprawling backwards.

Hengist nodded, then his eyes glazed over and he died, staring blankly up at the sky. Corvus muttered under his breath, "Farewell, Hengist. Perhaps we shall meet again in Valhalla."

Cradling her father's body, Merewyn let out a wail of grief. She remained like that for a short while, during which time Corvus killed two more Vikings. Then Merewyn picked herself up, a look of grim hatred in her eyes, and readied her bow. She would make them pay for killing her father if she could. But by now the Saxon shield line was breaking up. Most of the warriors were down, and the Vikings had broken through. Saxon and Viking bodies littered the ground, but the Saxons were hopelessly outnumbered. Some of the villagers were still fighting back to back, but it would be all over very soon.

Cearl was next. He went down under a flurry of Viking spears and axes, covered in wounds, fighting to the last. With his death the fight went out of the surviving Saxons. They tried to surrender, but many were slaughtered where they stood, the Viking bloodlust still too high for them to take prisoners.

But not Corvus. He had an oath to fulfil. And anyway, he had a policy of never surrendering. "To me, Merewyn," he shouted, "Get down behind me!"

Soon, Corvus and Merewyn were all that was left. Corvus began to swing his great axe over his head, a whirling circle of iron-edged death. Merewyn crouched behind him, firing her bow at those who threatened Corvus from behind. A few brave Vikings tried to rush in, but Corvus' axe shattered their shields and skulls like paper lanterns.

Soon all was silent, except for the sound of Corvus' breathing and his great axe singing its song of death. The Slaughter Wolves eyed him carefully. None would enter the circle to hear that song, for it would be the last song they would ever hear. But they could wait. Eventually he would tire.

Around them, the rest of Wulfric's men destroyed the village. Houses and buildings were torched, goods and money plundered. Women and children were shackled and led away to be sold as slaves. The remaining Saxon men who weren't too badly wounded were also shackled. Those too wounded to be worth anything were simply butchered where they lay. Wotanhirst was finished.

Two mounted Vikings rode up, and the Slaughter Wolves parted to allow them through. One carried the battle banner of Wulfric, a red flag with the head of a snarling she-wolf at bay, fangs bared and bloody. The rider wore a full helmet of fine workmanship inlaid with silver tracery, covering his features completely. The visor itself was shaped like a face, blank and expressionless. All that could be seen of the standard-bearer's own face was the faint glitter of his eyes behind the engraved steel. His armour was of strange design, as if from a bygone age. Segmented steel bands encased his chest and belly and banded shoulder guards covered his upper arms. He wore a leather kilt with steel shin guards beneath. The other rider was tall in the saddle, mounted on a great black mare, wearing no helmet at all. Red-haired and clean-shaven on the chin, he wore a great moustache that hung down on either side of his face, beaded and braided. He was strikingly handsome, but with a cruel twist to his mouth. This was Wulfric Cold-blood, in the flesh.

Still swinging his axe, Corvus stared at Wulfric, working things through. Could he get there in time to kill Wulfric before his men could bring him down? If only he had his two axes, he could have hurled them to deadly effect. But even if he had, Corvus remembered he couldn't kill Wulfric yet, anyway. First he had to find out where his sisters were.

Wulfric eyed Corvus, sizing him up. Then he signalled to his archers. "Why waste any more of my men on you when these lads can do it from fifty paces, eh?" he said, with a chilling smile.

It was this smile, among other things, that had earned Wulfric his nickname: Cold-blood. It was said that the sight of that smile made the blood run cold, for it always presaged bloody murder.

Corvus smiled back, a grim smile that was a mirror to Wulfric's own. That actually shook Wulfric for a moment. He halted the archers with a wave of the hand.

"Who are you? Tell us, that we might know the name of the mighty warrior we are forced to kill from afar," said Wulfric.

Corvus thought for a moment. It was obvious Wulfric didn't recognise him, and why should he? They had never met, though he had known of his father's sworn enemy since childhood. If he told Wulfric who he really was, he was dead. Maybe there was still a chance of talking his way out of this. Unlikely, but still a chance. Things had calmed down, and the bloodlust had faded. Men were always quieter after the rush of battle-slaughter had faded. At the least, perhaps he could get Merewyn sold into slavery rather than killed out of hand. That might be the best he could do to fulfil his oath to Hengist.

Corvus stilled his axe at last, resting it on the ground and leaning on it. Merewyn stood just behind him, looking at Corvus in surprise. The Viking warriors narrowed their eyes, ready to charge, but Wulfric kept them in check, like a hunt master with his hounds.

"I am Karfves Gunnarson of Gotland, called 'Blood-axe' by some. I think you can see why," said Corvus. The real Karfves "Blood-axe" Gunnarson was actually dead and no relation to Corvus. But Wulfric's mother, Kelda, had thought Corvus was dead and not Karfves, and so had Orm. Why not keep up the deception? Corvus congratulated himself inside. It was really quite a clever choice, he thought, a cunning ruse, worthy of Loki himself, the trickster god of Asgard.

"You're a Viking, then – I should have known. Karfves Gunnarson. Didn't you serve in the court of the king of Denmark, and fight at the battle of Lokr's Keep?" said Wulfric.

"Aye, that's me," said Corvus.

"You'll know this man, then," said Wulfric, gesturing arrogantly with one hand to summon someone from the Viking ranks.

A stocky warrior, short and bullish, stepped out

from the line to stand beside Wulfric. He lifted up his helm, revealing a pasty face with a sparse, raggedy beard and small piggy eyes, glowering at Corvus from under a wide, heavy forehead.

Corvus' heart sank. It was Ragnar Oath-breaker, who had served with Corvus and Karfves in the army of the king of Denmark. They'd both been with Karfves when he was killed at the battle of Lokr's Keep a year ago. There was no way Ragnar could fail to recognise Corvus, nor forget that it was really Karfves and not Corvus who was buried on some faraway Danish field. Ragnar had deserted soon after the battle, after stealing gold and silver arm-rings from the king's treasury, which was how he'd earned the name 'Oath-breaker'. Perhaps it wasn't a good idea to call him that to his face, thought Corvus. Obviously he'd found a kindred spirit in Wulfric.

Corvus sighed. Maybe he wasn't so clever after all. It was over – Wulfric would have him killed once he knew who he really was. He thought again of his twin axes, his brothers in battle. He could have tried a double throw, buried an axe in each skull – he might just have been able to take Wulfric and Ragnar with him.

Ragnar was staring at him. Surely he must recognise me, thought Corvus. They'd served together in the same unit for several years, fought side by side at the battle of Lokr's Keep.

Wulfric looked down at Ragnar inquisitively. "Well?" he said. Ragnar flicked his eyes up at Wulfric and then back at Corvus, silent, brooding. Suddenly he smiled broadly.

"Hello, Karfves," said Ragnar. "Good to see you again!"

Corvus thought furiously. Of course Ragnar knew who he was, but for some reason he wasn't telling Wulfric. Ragnar had always been a treacherous, self-serving schemer, and he was clearly up to something. Best play along until he could find out more.

"Ragnar, my old friend!" said Corvus. He grimaced inwardly. He was no friend. In fact, he really didn't like Ragnar. Not many people did. He was a liar, a traitor, a thief and an oath-breaker, after all. "It's good to see you too!"

Ragnar nodded and looked up at Wulfric. "Karfves Gunnarson," he said somewhat lamely, gesturing at Corvus.

"Yes, yes, I know that, you idiot," Wulfric said dismissively. No love lost between those two, thought Corvus.

Wulfric thought for a moment or two, still sitting on his horse. Then he asked, "So, what's a Norse reaver like you doing fighting with the Saxons?"

"For money," said Corvus simply.

"Money? Just you on your own?"

Corvus thought fast. "I was supposed to raise a band of mercenaries for them. To fight you, I think."

"To fight me, you say? Why?" said Wulfric.

"Cearl – their chief – was suspicious," Corvus said. "He thought Oslac was a fool to try and buy peace with you. He thought there'd be trouble. Guess he was right, eh?" Corvus chuckled.

Wulfric bared his chilling smile. "I suppose he was – and look where it got him," he said, nodding in the direction of Cearl's hall. Impaled on a stake was Cearl's head, tongue lolling, his beard stained scarlet with blood. Corvus raged inside – Cearl had been a good man, and deserved better. This was another crime that Wulfric would pay for one day. But right now, he couldn't let Wulfric know what he was thinking.

Corvus shrugged, trying to play the part of an unconcerned sword for hire. "He gambled. He lost," he said laconically.

Wulfric considered this. "Why did you fight so hard for these farmers?" he asked.

"Hard? I just fought like I always do. A contract's a contract. They paid me, I fought," said Corvus matter-of-factly.

"Even against these odds?"

"Aye," said Corvus nonchalantly. "I'd never get much work if I didn't honour my contracts, now, would I?"

Wulfric grunted, surprised, but he seemed to buy it. The mounted man carrying the battle banner, Wulfric's standard-bearer, leant over and whispered in his ear. When he'd finished, Wulfric narrowed his eyes and stared at Corvus, twirling his long, beaded moustache.

"We lost a fine champion today, a good shield-wall breaker and killer of men," he said.

"Aye. I'm sorry about that," said Corvus. "But that's what happens in battle. We'll all go down under the axe one of these days. And he died well – there'll be a place waiting for him in Valhalla." He was rather enjoying playing the uncaring mercenary.

"I need someone to replace him, a good killer," said Wulfric carefully.

"As it happens, my last contract has just run out," said Corvus. "Due to the unforeseen death of my employer," he added with a grin.

That caused a ripple of laughter among several of the Vikings. Others glowered, perhaps thinking of comrades who had died today at Corvus' hands. Some looked at him with interest, undoubtedly seeing a cold-hearted battle-skilled mercenary who could well save many of them from death in the future.

Wulfric observed everything. Nothing escaped his attention. At last he spoke. "Fight for me, then. You start on the same pay as the others, and an equal share of the loot, but if you distinguish yourself like you did today, you'll get a champion's cut – three times the ordinary share."

Corvus shrugged. "Fine by me," he said. And that was that.

Walking over to Wulfric, Corvus spat on his palm and offered it up. Wulfric spat too, and they clasped hands. Although filled with revulsion at Wulfric's touch, Corvus was exultant. He had fooled Wulfric completely, and now he could work against him, find out where his sisters were and then take his revenge.

Out of the corner of his eye, he could see Ragnar Oath-breaker looking at him, the ghost of a cynical smile on his lips.

And what of Merewyn? Her hands bound and her feet hobbled, she was led off, swearing and cursing like a wildcat, to join the remaining villagers. She was to be what the Norse called a *thrall*, a slave, destined to work in Wulfric's settlement or, more likely, to be sold for hard cash. There was little Corvus could do to help her at the moment without blowing his cover. Why would a hard-bitten mercenary care about a Saxon slave? But at least she was unlikely to be harmed, if she behaved herself. As she passed, she turned to Corvus and spat at him. "Traitor!" she yelled to his face.

The Vikings laughed at her rage, cuffing the girl into silence. Merewyn's display helped to back up his story, but inside, Corvus' stomach churned. From Merewyn's point of view what else could his behaviour be but treachery, and after he'd sworn to protect her? Yet to be a slave was the best protection she had. They wouldn't hurt her – she was worth too much. It was the best Corvus could do under the circumstances.

CHAPTER 8

RAGNAR OATH-BREAKER

The Slaughter Wolves were busy setting up camp in the burnt-out remains of Wotanhirst. Tonight they'd sleep in the ruins, then tomorrow head back for Ulfrsheim, Wulfric's settlement to the north. Some two days' march away, its name meant 'wolf's home' in the Norse language.

In the meantime, Wulfric ordered Ragnar to show Corvus the ropes. Ragnar was a captain, in charge of fifty men. He introduced Corvus to various officers and the troop of men he'd be staying with. To Corvus they seemed like an unruly bunch of thugs and murderers, the worst kind of Vikings. But they eyed Corvus with respect – they'd seen him in battle and knew him to be a mighty warrior. Most welcomed him in a friendly enough fashion, glad he was on their side now, though one or two were taciturn and surly, probably remembering friends and comrades that Corvus had cut down. But Corvus didn't expect this to be a problem for long. Men like this lived only for the moment, looking forward to the next chance for loot and plunder, for murder and mayhem. They didn't harbour grudges for long.

When the formalities were done, Ragnar found a chance to take Corvus aside, behind the wreckage of Cearl's hall, out of earshot of the men.

They stood silently for a moment, Ragnar with a slight, contemptuous smile on his lips, Corvus stony-faced and cautious, intent on giving nothing away until he could find out more about Ragnar's intentions.

After a few moments Ragnar said, "I know who you really are."

"Of course you do," said Corvus.

"And I know that Wulfric killed your family," Ragnar added. Corvus simply nodded. Ragnar frowned, perhaps thinking Corvus was not being very cooperative.

"So what are you doing here, then, pretending to be a dead man?" asked Ragnar.

Corvus waved his hand airily and shrugged, saying nothing. Ragnar could not be trusted, and Corvus wasn't going to tell him anything unless he had to.

Ragnar narrowed his eyes. "You'd better tell me what's going on, Corvus, or I'll tell Wulfric who you really are, and it'll be the Blood Eagle for you!" he said.

The Blood Eagle was an especially horrific Viking torture. The victim was cut open and his ribcage broken and spread apart like the wings of an eagle. It could take hours, even days to die. In agony.

Corvus raised an eyebrow and smiled. "No doubt it would be death for me, but what would Wulfric do to you? A man who lied to him about who I really was, who deceived him? It'd be the Blood Eagle for us both, I'd wager."

Ragnar cursed. Corvus was right. He stared at

Corvus, scratching his thin, raggedy beard.

"You're here to kill Wulfric, aren't you?" he said.

Corvus said nothing.

Exasperated, Ragnar went on, "I know you, Corvus. Vengeance and all that blood-feud honour stuff. You *must* want him dead."

Corvus shrugged. "Perhaps."

"Pah!" Ragnar barked in frustration. "You're as cagey as an oily merchant! I want him dead too, by Loki's arse!"

"Go on," said Corvus noncommittally.

Ragnar pursed his lips angrily. "We could work together, you and I. I've got friends within the war band – I could take over. Help me kill Wulfric and then stick around long enough to make sure I'm made the new leader. You get your revenge, and once I'm in charge, I'll throw in a bonus. You look like you could do with some cash."

Corvus knitted his brow in thought. He really wanted to kill Wulfric himself. What if it was Ragnar who finished Wulfric off? Corvus would feel robbed. Also, he couldn't really kill Wulfric until he'd found out where his sisters were.

Rescuing them had to be his priority, more important than his personal feelings of vengeance. But if he didn't go along with Ragnar's plan, then Ragnar would see Corvus as a threat. No, it'd be a recipe for bad blood, and Corvus didn't need that right now. He'd have to lie.

He nodded. "I'll help you," he said. "Together we'll get rid of him. Then I'll help you take over the war band."

Ragnar grinned in response. Corvus was easily the single best warrior he had ever known. With Corvus on his side the odds of succeeding in this highly risky endeavour were increased substantially. And once he was in charge, well, that was another matter. It wasn't good to be beholden to another man for too long.

Corvus looked down at his ill-fitting leather armour and tattered clothes. "I need some fresh equipment. Mail shirt, and two axes, not too big, not too small," he said.

"Of course!" Ragnar said enthusiastically, happy to oblige now that he had Corvus on board. "I remember your axes – Corvus 'Twin-axe' we used to call you. And a champion of the Slaughter Wolves should have some decent armour and a good shield. I'll see what I can do."

"And new boots, clothes and a warm cloak," Corvus added quickly.

Ragnar raised his eyes, "All right, all right." He looked Corvus up and down. "If I can find some to fit you. Mind you, we took more casualties than we expected – thanks to you – so there's plenty of spare gear," he added with a wry smile.

"Good – I'll need it if we're to succeed in our plan," said Corvus.

Ragnar nodded. "Yes, true enough. For now, you should settle in with your unit, find a place to bed down. I'll be round to see you with your gear later."

As Ragnar turned to go, Corvus said, "Hold on a moment. I don't suppose you know what happened to my sisters, do you?"

"Sisters? I didn't know you had any. Haven't heard anything about sisters either, nor any talk about them in camp. Mind you, the whole Gunnarson 'House Party', as Wulfric called it, was before my time. Do you want me to ask Wulfric?"

Gunnarson House Party – that's what Wulfric called the murder of his family, did he? Corvus felt his blood boil. Well, he'd give Wulfric a party he wouldn't forget, that was for sure. And he'd invite any of the Slaughter Wolves who'd been involved. Corvus began to go through the various ways he could kill Wulfric, and how good it would feel.

"Well," said Ragnar, interrupting his train of thought, "do you want me to ask Wulfric or not?"

"No!" said Corvus. "That would be far too suspicious."

"Good point," said Ragnar. "These sisters of yours. Good-looking, are they?" he said, licking his lips and leering unpleasantly.

Corvus just stared at him; a hard, cold stare. Ragnar had a terrible reputation with women, violent and cruel. What's more, he knew Ragnar was lying: Corvus' parents had been killed too recently for Ragnar not to have been a part of Wulfric's war band.

Ragnar coughed and looked away. Then he turned and left, leaving Corvus brooding in the smoking ruins of Cearl's hall, once vibrant with laughter and song, now blackened and broken, a place of desolation and despair.

CHAPTER 9

THE WAR GOD'S SHRINE

It was early evening on the following day. Corvus was sitting by a fire, watching a cauldron bubble with a stew of chicken and vegetables. Food was plentiful now that Wotanhirst had been sacked. Around him were several Viking *drengs* – young warriors – the men of his troop. There were twelve men in a troop, organised according to the number of oarsmen on a Viking longboat, usually six benches' worth of men, two oarsmen to a bench. This troop had been reduced to only nine men. Probably some of that was due to him.

The day had been spent on the march, tramping through the dusty Saxon countryside under a hot summer sun. Corvus hadn't seen hide nor hair of Ragnar since their meeting in Wotanhirst yesterday, and his feet were sore after a day's march with only a pair of tattered Saxon leathers as shoes. So much for Ragnar's promise of new equipment.

Still, he'd managed to check on Merewyn – that was something. She was corralled with the rest of the Saxon prisoners, shuffling along at the back of the column, hobbled, but at least well fed and watered. The Slaughter Wolves wouldn't mistreat the Saxons unless they caused trouble – not out of kindness or compassion, but because the better their condition when they were sold as slaves, the better the price. Corvus had managed to exchange a glance with Merewyn so she would know he hadn't forgotten her, but all he'd got in return was a cold stare.

As Corvus considered Merewyn's fate, he spotted Ragnar making his way over to the campfire, carrying a heavy sack on his shoulders. The men eyed him warily. Ragnar was not liked. He would use any excuse to come down on them hard, too hard, and usually for his own enjoyment rather than for the betterment of the men as a fighting unit.

But Ragnar ignored the looks and walked over to Corvus, dumping the sack rudely at his feet, before giving him a nod and walking off without a word. The men were now eyeing the sack curiously.

Corvus opened it and drew out a set of good solid leather boots; a grimy old cloak, tattered but still serviceable; a pair of iron-headed axes; and a set of worn leather armour – breastplate, greaves and vambraces – as well as a heavy leather belt with a built-in pouch.

"Hey," Corvus shouted after Ragnar, "I thought you were going to get me a mail shirt!"

Ragnar stopped in his tracks. The men around Corvus waited expectantly. This was exactly the sort of thing that would trigger one of Ragnar's rages.

"You're for it now, Karfves," someone whispered.

Ragnar turned and stared at Corvus. "You think mail shirts grow on trees, do you?" he said evenly. Then his voice began to rise. "Do you know how much a mail shirt costs? Where am I supposed to get one – thin air? One in fifty of us have mail, by Loki's arse! Even I haven't got one, and I'm a *captain*!"

Ragnar was shouting now, spittle flying from his lips. Corvus simply raised an eyebrow. Ragnar huffed grumpily, rather like an old woman. "You'll have to earn your mail shirt, know what I mean?" he said. With that, he turned and continued on his way.

"Hooo, you were lucky. Talking to Ragnar like that would normally get you a week's worth of latrine duty!" said one of the men, a grizzled old thug with pink, lurid scars where his ears had been. Corvus knew that cropping the ears was a common punishment for persistent cattle rustling and thievery.

"Well, Ragnar and I go back a long way," said Corvus.

"What?" said Crop-ears. That would be a good name for the thug, Corvus decided.

"I said... oh, forget it," Corvus said, examining the axes. They were well-honed and in excellent condition. The right size for him, too – good for throwing and for hand-to-hand combat, though most men weren't strong enough to use them the way Corvus could. As he was testing their weight, Corvus noticed a piece of paper wrapped around the handle of one of the axes. A message from Ragnar!

Nonchalantly, Corvus went through his gear, as if giving it the once-over. With his back to the men, he unwrapped the paper. There was something written on it in runes. Corvus groaned inside. He wasn't a good reader, especially with the runes. His Latin was better, thanks to his mother, but even then he was barely literate. It'd be an effort to de-cipher this, and he could hardly ask someone else to read it for him.

The first word was easy enough. It was his name.

ᚲᚩᚱᚢᚢᛋ ᚷᚢᛏᛏᚪᚱᛋᚩᚾ

'Corvus Gunnarson'

He began to work on the second line.

ᛏᛟᛞᛁᛦ ᛁᛋ ᛏᛁᚹᛋᛞᛁᛦ

'Today is Tiwsday'

Today is, what, Tiwsday or Tuesday? Well, of course it was. By Thor's hammer, Ragnar didn't have to tell him that, Corvus thought. The next few lines looked like this.

ᛏᛁᚹ ᛁᛋ ᛏᚻᛗ ᛋᚨ☐ᛟᚾ ᚷᛟᛞ ᛟᚠ ᚹᚨᚱ, ᛏᚻᛗ
ᛋᚨᛈᛗ ᛁᛋ ᛟᚢᚱ ᚢᛁᚲᛁᚾᚷ ᚷᛟᛞ ᛟᚠ ᚹᚨᚱ, ᛏᛦᚱ.

'Tiw is the Saxon god of war, the same
as our Viking god of war, Tyr.'

Tiw and Tyr. What was this – a lesson in the Viking and Saxon gods? Slowly he deciphered the next few lines.

ᚹᚢᛚᚠᚱᛁᚲ ᚹᛟᚱᛋᚻᛁᚲᛋ ᛏᛦᚱ. ᛏᚻᛗᚱᛗ ᛁᛋ ᚨ
ᛋᚨᚲᛋᛟᚾ ᛋᚻᚱᛁᛏᛗ ᛏᛟ ᛏᛁᚹ ᚨᛏ ᛏᚻᛗ ᛟᛏᚻᛗᚱ
ᛋᛁᛞᛗ ᛟᚠ ᚻᚨᚷᛋᚻᛗᚨᛞ ᚻᛁᛚᛚ.

*'Wulfric worships Tyr. There is a Saxon shrine
to Tiw on the other side of Hagshead Hill.'*

Corvus scratched his head. Where, by the
sleet-cold halls of Hel, was Hagshead Hill? And why
should he care? He sighed and struggled on.

ᛚᛟᛟᚲ ᚢᛈ ᚨᚾᛞ ᛃᛟᚢ'ᛚᛚ ᛋᛖᛖ ᛏᚺᛖ ᚺᛁᛚᛚ ᛁ
ᛗᛖᚨᚾ. ᛗᛖᛖᛏ ᛗᛖ ᛏᚺᛖᚱᛖ ᚨᛋ ᛋᛟᛟᚾ ᚨᛋ
ᛃᛟᚢ ᚲᚨᚾ. ᚹᚢᛚᚠᚱᛁᚲ ᚹᛁᛚᛚ ᛒᛖ ᛟᚾ ᚺᛁᛋ ᛟᚹᚾ,
ᚲᚱᚨᛃᛁᚾᚷ.

*'Look up and you'll see the hill I mean.
Meet me at the shrine as soon as you can.
Wulfric will be on his own, praying.
We can kill him there.
Ragnar'*

Ah, now I get it, Corvus thought. On his own,
the perfect time to kill him. He frowned. He'd
better get on over there – there was no telling what
Ragnar would do, especially if things went wrong
and Wulfric got the better of him. He'd have no

compunction about telling Wulfric who Corvus really was to save his own skin.

Corvus scanned the nearby horizon. He spotted the hill in question, a rocky outcrop that did indeed look like the head of a hag with a long, warty nose, wrinkled old lips and crooked teeth, formed out of a jumble of boulders. Buckling on the heavy belt, Corvus stashed the note in the leather pouch and put on his leather boots. Then, slinging his new axes over his shoulder, he set off for the hill.

"Where are you off to so quick, Karfves?" asked a warrior who was ladling stew into wooden bowls, "I'm just serving up dinner!"

"Er – sudden call of nature, boys!" said Corvus, clutching his belly.

This caused a ripple of laughter from the men. "Try not to drink so much mead next time," someone called.

Crop-ears looked up at the commotion. "What was that? Time for mead, is it?" he said. This set off a further round of laughter, which suited Corvus as it kept them occupied while he made off for the hill.

As soon as he was out of sight of the camp, Corvus set a fast pace, eating up the distance to the hill in great strides. Soon he crested the ridge of Hagshead Hill. Below him he saw a bowl of lush green woodland surrounded by low hills. Nestled at the foot of the hill was a large pond, fed by a spring bubbling out of a pile of rocks. Natural springs of this sort were often seen as sacred by Saxons and Vikings alike. A path that led from the ridge down to the spring had been cut through the wood. It ran up to a small stone pillar inscribed with runes, and an altar stained with the blood of many animal sacrifices. Here was the shrine of Tiw or Tyr, the war god.

In the dying light, Corvus could see Wulfric bowed over the altar, his hands resting on the cold stone plinth, no doubt praying to his patron god. Tyr had a nickname: 'the leavings of the Wolf'. This was because Tyr had had his hand bitten off by Fenrir, the great wolf of the gods, who was destined to eat Odin whole at Ragnarök, the battle at the end of time. A war god with a wolf connection. Who else would Wulfric choose as his favoured god?

As quietly as he could, Corvus began to make his way down to the shrine. As he drew near, he spotted Ragnar skulking behind a tree, not ten paces from Wulfric! With a sword in one hand and a dagger in the other, he was staring intently at Wulfric's back, probably steeling himself to make a rush for it. Every now and then Ragnar looked back at Hagshead Hill, scanning the horizon. Corvus grinned to himself. Ragnar would wait for him – he didn't have the guts to try it on his own.

Then Ragnar saw Corvus, and his face lit up with an unholy glee. Comically he put a finger to his lips, signalling for quiet, as if Corvus didn't know that already. Then he drew his dagger across the front of his throat, and nodded towards Wulfric. Corvus paused, unsure. He probably could take Wulfric now, but he wanted to do it face to face, to look Wulfric in the eye and let him know who had killed him and why. There was also the far more pressing problem of his sisters. Knowledge of their whereabouts would die with Wulfric, unless he could get it out of him first. Wulfric was a murderous villain, a cruel, evil man, but he was no coward. He wouldn't respond to threats. Even torture was unlikely to break him, and in any case, Corvus wasn't the torturing kind. What to do?

Ragnar became more frantic, nodding vigorously towards Wulfric and pretending to cut his throat. Still Corvus stood there, trapped in his dilemma. This drove Ragnar wild. He took his sword, and mimed driving it through his belly, nodding at Wulfric. In the end, he couldn't help himself, and he hissed angrily under his breath, "Do him now, you idiot!"

Suddenly Wulfric straightened and cocked his head. He'd heard that angry hiss! It was now or never for Ragnar. With a strangled cry he dashed out of hiding, in a desperate attempt to bring Wulfric down before his leader found out he was there.

Wulfric turned. His jaw dropped and his eyes widened in shock as Ragnar charged in, uttering a blood-curdling scream. Wulfric was at his mercy. Without thinking, Corvus reached up to grasp the hafts of his twin axes and hurled them both, as quick as lightning.

The first struck Ragnar directly in the back of his skull, the second in the nape of his neck, killing him instantly. Ragnar's cry was shut off in mid-shriek, and he toppled forward, dead before he hit the ground.

Wulfric flinched as a spray of blood spattered his face. He stared in astonishment at the mess of Ragnar's head. Then he looked up to see Corvus.

"By Tyr's hand... you? What...? Why...?" was all he could say.

Corvus groaned inwardly. He had no choice; he'd just saved Wulfric's life. He had to find out where his sisters were before Wulfric could die. He thought fast. He'd have to make this convincing.

"I thought he was up to no good," he said conversationally.

Wulfric wiped Ragnar's blood from his face, cleaning his hands on the grass. "Treachery!" he said.

"I saw him head off this way, skulking like a dog, sword and dagger at his side. I thought it was a bit odd so I followed him. Lucky I did, eh?"

Wulfric looked Corvus up and down, as if seeing him in a new light. Then a frown of suspicion appeared on his brow.

"Lucky indeed," he said. "What made you think he'd be coming here to murder me? With a knife in the back, no less, the cowardly cur!" Wulfric leant forward and spat on Ragnar's still-twitching corpse. Then he reached down and picked up Corvus' battle-brothers, one in each hand. "How did you know he had black murder in his heart?"

"Ah, well, I've known Ragnar for years, so it was no surprise to me," Corvus said.

The laconic reply worked. Wulfric burst out laughing. He strode over to Corvus, took both axes in one hand, and clapped him on the back with the other.

"They didn't call him Oath-breaker for nothing, you know," Corvus added.

Wulfric chuckled. He handed Corvus his axes, any suspicions he might have had well and truly allayed. They started back to camp. Wulfric was silent, deep in thought. Corvus' mind, too, was whirling.

Then Wulfric broke the silence.

"You saved my life, Karfves," he said. "This one'll make a good story for the campfires and mead halls, I'll make sure of that!"

"That's what you pay me for," said Corvus jovially, even though inside he was seething, wanting nothing more than to tear out Wulfric's throat.

Wulfric looked at Corvus. "This is more than I expect for a day's pay, Karfves. You've gone up in my estimation, indeed you have."

"Just doing my job," said Corvus, trying not to shudder at the touch of Wulfric's arm across his shoulder. This man had killed his mother and father, by Odin's fury!

"More than just your job, Karfves. You and I, we could go far together. I need a man like you, a killer I can trust," said Wulfric.

"Aye, glad to be of service, sir," said Corvus.

"Call me Wulfric. You've earned that."

As they reached the camp, the sun began to go down behind Hagshead Hill, and a reddish glow filled the sky, like an omen of blood.

"Get a good night's sleep, and come and see me

tomorrow morning, Karfves," said Wulfric. "I want to think about how to reward you for this evening's work. And don't worry, I shall be generous."

With a final slap on the back, Wulfric departed, heading for his tent in the centre of the Slaughter Wolves' encampment. Corvus headed over to his troop, somewhat bemused at the turn of events, and very much hoping that supper was waiting for him.

CHAPTER 10

BLOOD BROTHERS

At daybreak the camp of the Slaughter Wolves began to stir. Breakfast was served – a typical Viking breakfast, with chunks of mutton floating in salted oat porridge.

As the men ate, the blast of a horn filled the air, its raucous cry summoning the men to a council outside the *Jarl's*, or chieftain's, tent.

The men hurriedly polished off their food and made their way to the centre of the camp, where Wulfric was waiting for them. He was mounted on his great black mare in full ceremonial armour, with polished helm, gleaming mail and many gold and silver rings on his upper arms, in "gold-bright splendour," as the *skalds*, the Viking bards, liked to say. Just behind him, similarly mounted, was his standard-bearer, dressed in his strange armour from a forgotten time, holding aloft the she-wolf battle banner of the Slaughter Wolves. As usual, the standard-bearer wore the strange helm that looked like a face, his true features obscured, silent, inscrutable.

As they drew near, the men could see a body impaled on a stake next to Wulfric, the badly mauled head virtually unrecognisable. But on closer inspection the raggedy beard and the clothes revealed that it was Ragnar Oath-breaker, impaled for all to see, food for the crows and the ravens, eaters of the dead.

The men arranged themselves in a semicircle in front of Wulfric, buzzing with rumours and wild guesses, eager to hear the tale behind the ending of Ragnar. Some of Wulfric's other captains seemed nervous, as if unsure of what this meant for them. Corvus shifted uncomfortably. He wasn't sure either.

Wulfric raised his hand, signalling for silence.

"My Wolves, my slaughter boys," he said. "I have a tale to tell! I want you all to hear my story of black-hearted treachery, of a hero and of a great deed!"

Wulfric paused for dramatic effect, and Corvus heard one man whisper, "It's always like this. He thinks he's a great *skald* or something,"

"Aye," said another. "It's obvious Ragnar tried something and got killed for it – why doesn't he just get on with things!"

Wulfric went on. "Ragnar Oath-breaker was true to his name. While I prayed to Tyr, the great god of war, our patron who guides us to victory in battle, this mangy dog of a traitor came against me. He sought to overthrow me, to make himself the ruler in my place!"

He paused again. Men shuffled nervously, unsure what they should do. Wulfric seemed surprised, as if he expected more of a reaction. He glowered angrily.

Some of the men picked up on this, and one shouted, "That snake-in-the-grass Ragnar!"

Others joined in. "May the queen of Hel suck the marrow from his bones!"

"Ragnar always was a traitor!"

"He won't make it to Valhalla!"

"Feed his corpse to the maggots!"

This seemed to mollify Wulfric. He went on.

"He crept up behind me in the dusk-time, in the shadows. And he would have slain me, too, with a dagger in the back, if it wasn't for another who saved me! A brave man, a true hero of the Slaughter Wolves, who struck the traitor down with an axe hurled with peerless skill, an axe that shattered the oath-breaker's turncoat skull like an egg!"

Wulfric stopped again. The men realised it was their cue, and they all cheered loudly.

"That man was Karfves 'Blood-axe' Gunnarson!" shouted Wulfric at the top of his voice. "Come here, Karfves, come here so that I may honour you!"

Corvus groaned inside. But what could he do? He'd have to play along. Grinning like a madman, he made his way to the front. The men parted around him, making way, surprised looks on their faces. Corvus could hear whispered words in the ranks.

"Right, so Ragnar tried to top Wulfric with a

knife in the back, and the new guy, Karfves, killed him for it," said one.

"Why didn't he just say so from the start instead of all that tosh?" said another.

"I know, it's always the same," replied the other.

"Oh for a *Jarl* of few words," said yet another, trying not to laugh.

"Shhh! If he hears you, it'll be the Blood Eagle, by Odin's beard!" whispered someone else.

As Corvus approached, Wulfric dismounted and put his arm, covered in mail, around him. Corvus tried not to grimace in disgust at the feel of Wulfric's arm across his shoulders.

"Now hear this, you Slaughter Wolves, you sons of mayhem! Karfves will take over from Ragnar, and will be the captain of fifty men! From now on, he will be my personal champion, my favoured warrior!"

He paused again for effect. The men cheered, right on cue this time.

Wulfric tried to smile benignly, but it came out as it always did – a smile that chilled the blood. The cheering died off and Wulfric turned to Corvus.

"So, my friend, what boon do you crave? Ask anything, and if it is in my power to grant it, I will do so! Let it not be said that Wulfric does not reward the faithful and the loyal!"

Corvus looked nervously from side to side. He really didn't want to be here. He couldn't think of anything to say, other than, "I want your black smoking heart on a plate, you murdering swine!" But somehow, that didn't seem like the best idea.

Wulfric's face darkened. "Well," he said, "what do you want?" Corvus had to give an answer or risk insulting Wulfric in front of his men. Then he had an idea.

"A *thrall*," he said, "to be my servant. I've always wanted one of those," he added, playing the not-so-bright mercenary to the hilt. Some of the men laughed at his simple request. Wulfric seemed pleased as well – he had slaves aplenty, so it was a nice, cheap reward.

"Easily done, my friend. We've got one or two right here in camp!" he said loudly, which caused another ripple of laughter among the men. "Anyone in particular?"

Corvus pretended to think. Then he said, "How about that Saxon archer from the village? What's her name, Merethyn? No, Merewyn, that was it! She'll do."

Smiling in what he thought was kingly beneficence but was in fact a cold, reptilian grin, Wulfric raised his arm and declaimed, "Bring forth the slave called Merewyn! She is now Karfves' property!"

Corvus allowed himself a small smile. Corvus could protect Merewyn far more easily as his own slave than if she belonged to someone else, especially a man like Wulfric. If he could kill Wulfric and get them out of here in one piece, he could set Merewyn free. If Hengist was listening in far-off Valhalla, he would be pleased that Corvus was keeping the oath he had made to him in his dying moments.

Merewyn was brought forward, hands bound in front of her, feet hobbled together with just enough rope so she could walk but not run. She stared coldly at Corvus, her thin, rangy body quivering with rage. "I heard everything," she hissed angrily.

Corvus blinked, confused. Didn't she realise he'd just saved her from a far worse fate? Or did she really think he'd gone over to the other side?

At that moment, some of the men began to stir, thinking the meeting was over, but Wulfric said, "Wait. There is one more thing. Karfves and I shall take the Blood Oath! We shall swear loyalty to each other; we shall become blood brothers!"

The men cheered on cue again. Merewyn nodded knowingly at Corvus, a look of disgust on her face, as if she'd expected this confirmation that Corvus had betrayed her. Corvus wanted to shake his head, to tell Merewyn the truth, but he couldn't do it in front of so many witnesses. Blood brothers! With his sworn enemy! And there was nothing he could do about it. To refuse would be a mortal insult at the best of times, but to refuse in front of Wulfric's men? He'd have no choice but to have Corvus killed, even if he didn't want to. Involuntarily, Corvus put his head in his hands, as if in despair.

Wulfric frowned. "Are you all right, Karfves?" he asked.

"What?" said Corvus, "Oh, yes, I'm fine, I'm just overwhelmed – I wasn't expecting this great honour, my lord," he said, straightening up quickly and smiling as if this was the happiest day of his life.

This seemed to satisfy Wulfric. He drew a dagger from his belt, cut himself on the palm of his hand, and handed the dagger to Corvus. As if in a dream – or a nightmare – Corvus did the same, though what he really wanted to do was to plunge the dagger into Wulfric's eyes. They clasped hands and together recited the words of the Viking Blood Oath, swearing loyalty each to the other until death and beyond. Corvus knew he'd never be free of this; the Blood Oath held even in Valhalla.

When it was over, the men, knowing their duty, cheered until Wulfric cut them short with a curt, irritable wave. Dismissing them, he gave orders that they should ready themselves for the march back to Ulfrsheim, a day's travel away. Quickly, he turned back to Corvus.

"Well, my brother, how's that for a reward, eh?"

"Grand, my lord, grand. A great day for Karfves!" said Corvus. "I'll be off, then, sir, to join my troop."

Wulfric laughed at that. "Your troop? You're my blood brother, by Odin, and a captain of fifty men now. You'll march with me with your men behind you, pride of place at the head of the column."

Corvus nodded. "Of course, my lord."

"You don't have to call me lord. Brother or just Wulfric will do, now that we're bound together by the Blood Oath." Wulfric laughed again and slapped Corvus on the back, leaving a bloody handprint behind.

Corvus wasn't sure he could bring himself to call Wulfric 'brother'. In fact, he wasn't sure of anything right now. Except for one thing. The Three Goddesses, the Norns, those weavers of men's destinies, had spun his fate as a twisted, tangled tale indeed.

CHAPTER 11

BAD BLOOD

The tramp of 250 pairs of boots and the jangle of war gear filled the air. The Slaughter Wolves were on the march. Ahead of Corvus, Wulfric and the standard-bearer, she-wolf banner held aloft, rode on horses. Corvus hadn't heard the standard-bearer say a single word since he'd joined the war band, nor had he ever seen his face.

Behind Corvus the rest of the Slaughter Wolves marched in a column four men wide, heading towards their fort along an old Roman road. They bore spears in hand, with swords and axes at their belts and shields slung on their backs. Their armour was hauled along behind them in carts or carried by slaves. Merewyn marched next to Corvus, carrying his armour slung over her shoulder in a sack.

"Traitor!" she'd hissed in Corvus' ear when they'd formed up the column. Since then, she hadn't said a word. That had angered Corvus, but there was little he could do about it while they were on the march, in full view of everyone.

As they marched on, Corvus reflected. He'd sworn an oath of vengeance against Wulfric. How could things have turned out like this? He'd saved his life, been named a high-ranking officer in his war band and had sworn a new oath as his blood brother. Not exactly a great success. Whatever he did now, he would end up being an oath-breaker like Ragnar. If he killed Wulfric, he would fulfil his vow of vengeance but break the sacred Blood Oath. If he let him live, he would fulfil the Blood Oath, but break the oath he had made to his ancestors, and to Odin, and to Ullr, the god of the blood feud.

He'd also sworn an oath to Hengist, and the woman he had promised to protect hated him and thought he was an oath-breaking, Hel-cursed traitor. Now there was bad blood between them, and he still had no idea where his sisters were; the sisters whom he'd also sworn an oath to protect. Things weren't going well.

But at that moment, Corvus' train of thought was interrupted by a horn blast. The standard-bearer had raised a horn to his lips and blown some kind of signal. He hadn't even lifted up his faceplate to do it. Behind him, the men came to a halt and began to fall out to the sides of the road. Boots were taken off and weary feet rubbed. Drinks were passed around and beef jerky was taken out and chewed. It was time for a break.

It was the perfect moment for Corvus to take Merewyn aside, and he managed to find a spot where they could talk quietly without being overheard. But when he leant over to speak to her, Merewyn turned away, as if she wasn't listening.

"If I've sold out to Wulfric, why do you think I'm going under an assumed name, by Thor's hammer?" whispered Corvus.

Merewyn frowned for a moment, conceding Corvus had a point. But then she reverted to her mask of angry disdain.

"Maybe there is bad blood between your family and his, but that changes nothing," Merewyn said furiously. "You saved his life! After you said you'd sworn an oath of vengeance against him. You lied to us! You lied to my father, you traitorous Viking murderer."

"No, you don't understand, Merewyn. I had no choice!" said Corvus.

"No choice!" Merewyn repeated. "You killed that Ragnar fellow, and now you've been promoted, been given gifts – blood brothers, for Jesus' sake! Is that how you keep your vows, eh?"

Corvus grabbed Merewyn's shirt and pulled her close. "By Odin's fury, I swear to you, I did what I had to do for your sake, and for the sake of my sisters!"

"Your sisters? What are you talking...?"

But suddenly they were interrupted by the sight of three Slaughter Wolf captains sauntering over. Each wore a wolf-head skin over his helmet.

"Karfves! Tell us the real story about that dog Ragnar!" said the first, a scarred Viking with a soft, wispy beard of prodigious length.

"Let's just say he had an unfortunate axi-dent," said Corvus.

All three burst out laughing. They sat down to hear the tale. Corvus told them what had happened between him, Ragnar and Wulfric. One of them asked the same question Wulfric had asked. "But how did you know what he was planning?" Corvus gave a similar answer – "I knew him well" – and got the same reaction, a chuckle of laughter.

Then the standard-bearer came by on his horse. The three men fell silent, looking up at him oddly, as if they were disturbed by his presence. The standard-bearer said nothing and simply trotted past, gesturing with the banner to right and left.

Corvus raised a questioning eyebrow.

"The signal that rest is over, time to get back on the march," explained the scarred captain with the wispy beard.

As the standard-bearer moved on, another captain made a sign of the evil eye with his fingers and spat, warding off evil. Corvus did the same.

The wisp-bearded Viking leant forward. "I've been with Wulfric for five years, and never have I heard the standard-bearer speak, nor seen his face," he whispered, getting to his feet. "Some say he is a demon in the armour of a man."

Merewyn crossed herself at this and Corvus fingered his amulet of Thor, mouthing a silent prayer to the thunder god. Then a thought came to him. The Viking with the wispy beard had said he'd been with Wulfric for five years. Almost certainly he'd been with him at the 'Gunnarson House Party' when they'd butchered his parents.

"What's your name, mate?" said Corvus, trying to keep the anger out of his voice.

"I'm Lars," the man said as he walked away. "Lars Silkbeard."

Maybe Lars knew where his sisters were, thought Corvus. Maybe he could get it out of him by force – before he killed him, for any part he might have played in the murder of his parents.

Merewyn stood up, angrily hefting her sack of armour.

"Wait," said Corvus, "Hear me out!"

"Back into line, *Captain*," said Merewyn, her voice filled with contempt as she walked off to take her place in the column.

Corvus had no choice but to follow.

CHAPTER 12

WOLVES AT BAY

Corvus marched on down the hot, dusty road at the head of his company. On the left, for league after league, a great forest seemed to march along beside them. Many men had walked this path over the centuries, from ancient Britons and Romans to Saxons and Jutes. Now it was the turn of the Vikings. War-stained shields and blades, helms and axes, iron and steel, back and forth in a seemingly never-ending dance of battle and strife – blood spilled, flesh torn, skulls split, all for wealth and glory and ownership of this green and pleasant land. How many had died, how many had watered the very earth they fought over with their blood?

Eventually the trees gave out and the company came to a broad pasture. No sheep or goats gently cropped the overgrown grasses. No shepherd watched over them, playing his flute under the summer sun, no peasants prepared the land for harvest. Where the forest came to an end, blackened farmhouses and barns leant drunkenly on shattered foundations, empty and abandoned. The Slaughter Wolves had plundered this place weeks ago on a previous visit, killing or enslaving the inhabitants, butchering the animals and salting their meat.

Across the pasture was a low stone wall that ran up to the banks of a swift-flowing river. Some way beyond the wall, a row of hills rose across the horizon. They were called the Suthduns by the Saxons.

Up ahead, a Viking outrider galloped frantically towards the company. As he neared the head of the column, he shouted, "Saxons! The Saxons are coming!"

"Calm down, man, or I'll have you gutted like a fish, by Odin!" said Wulfric loudly. The outrider drew his horse up short, gulping fearfully.

"So what if the Saxons are coming?" Wulfric went

on. "We'll cut them down just like the last lot!"

Some of the men chuckled. But the outrider said, "No, my lord, I mean a Saxon army, led by King Oslac himself!"

As if to underscore his words, across the ridgeline of the Suthduns a row of glittering spearheads appeared, closely followed by gleaming helms and brightly painted shields, hundreds of them. Without breaking their stride, the Saxons began to pace with measured tread down the side of the hill towards the Viking Slaughter Wolves.

For a moment, Wulfric gaped in astonishment, probably wondering how Oslac had known where to find him.

"He has a hundred Huscarls and at least five hundred men of the *fyrd*, my lord!" said the Viking outrider.

Wulfric's eyes narrowed at talk of the Huscarls – King Oslac's elite bodyguard – and the *fyrd*, the Saxon army, raised from farmers and peasants.

"To that wall! Draw up a shield wall: anchor our right flank on the river, our left at that ruined farm and the forest," yelled Wulfric. "Break out the armour – we've just enough time to gear up before they reach us!"

With admirable discipline and speed, the Vikings ran for the low wall, drawing themselves up for battle in ordered lines, shields locked together, spears and axes at the ready. Hurriedly the carts were brought up; *thralls* and squires handed out armour and weapons to each unit. The recently captured Saxon slaves were tied and hobbled in the rear, a couple of guards assigned to keep them in place. Wulfric took up a position in the centre of the line, just behind his best troops, his standard-bearer alongside him. Corvus found himself in a similar position behind his own men on the right flank. Merewyn was beside him, helping him to put on his armour like a good slave.

"Horsa!" she hissed triumphantly into Corvus' ear.

"What do you mean?" said Corvus, suspicious she was insulting him.

"Horsa, you fool! Cearl's son. He sent him to Oslac, remember? Looks like he made it through. Now you Viking scum will pay for your crimes," she said, looking up at the Saxon army, her eyes shining with pride.

"Ah," said Corvus. "Of course." He remembered what Cearl had said when he'd sent his son riding to the king: "*Tell him to bring his army, and don't let the Vikings catch you!*"

"Hmm. Looks like Cearl will have the victory after all, even in death. Good for him, he deserves it," said Corvus as he buckled on his greaves.

Merewyn looked at Corvus strangely. "They'll show you no quarter," she said.

"Aye, well, can't say they deserve any, not after what they did at Wotanhirst, eh?"

Just then a horn blast rent the air. Wulfric bellowed at the top of his voice, "Captains to me!"

Leaving Merewyn with the other slaves, Corvus moved over to where Wulfric stood along with Lars Silkbeard and two other captains whose names he didn't know.

"They outnumber us at least two to one," said Wulfric. "That means they'll have a longer shield wall and could outflank us. Our right flank is protected by the river. Our problem is the left. They might try sending a force through the ruined farms to get behind our line."

The men nodded in agreement. Wulfric knew his stuff when it came to battles.

"Corvus, my brother, take half your men and hold the farmhouses and barns," Wulfric continued. "Prevent them breaking through. If they try and skirt it, cut them off. You have to stop them no matter what the cost. If they break through, we're dead. The rest of you, as you were."

With that, he dismissed his captains back to their posts. As they walked away, Wulfric began to chant.

"Spears will shatter, shields will splinter, swords will gnaw like wolves through armour." Then he grinned, a feral grin of bloodlust and delight. Wulfric loved war, slaughter and mayhem. It was what he lived for.

"Good line – did he make it up himself?" asked one of the captains.

"By Odin, no! He fancies himself a *skald* but he can't compose a line. No, that's from Njal's Saga," said Lars Silkbeard. "He says it before every battle."

Corvus picked twenty-five of his best men as well as Merewyn, and headed over to the ruined farm, fingering his amulet and thinking furiously. He could not arm Merewyn without arousing suspicion, but he could keep her with him. What to do? During the ensuing fight, all would be chaos. He could certainly find a moment to kill Wulfric. Or maybe better – find Lars Silkbeard, and get the fate of his sisters out of him, kill him and then kill Wulfric. But what if Lars didn't know? No, he still needed Wulfric alive. He was going to have to play it by ear, see what happened.

Corvus distributed his men as sensibly as possible among the ruined buildings. In a gap between two walls, he drew up ten of them, two deep to cover the space. For the rest of the men it would have to be bitter, house-to-house fighting. Then he took himself up to the attic of a roofless barn, where he could get a good all-round view of the battle. Merewyn climbed up behind him.

As the Saxons drew near, Wulfric bellowed a short speech to his men.

"Slaughter Wolves! We're such a thorn in the

Saxon side that King Oslac himself has come to deal with us. He has a hundred Huscarls with him, mighty warriors, trained from boyhood in the axe and spear. He also has hundreds of *fyrd*men, spear-armed and eager to taste revenge! It's true they outnumber us two to one. But most of his army are peasants! Farmers! Fodder for good Viking weapons, grain to be reaped by our iron sword-scythes. They don't even count! That leaves a hundred Huscarls, well-matched man-for-man with hard-bitten Viking veterans like us. But there are two hundred and fifty of us, each one a seasoned warrior, as good as any Huscarl. That means we outnumber *them* two to one!"

This caused a storm of laughter among the men. Wulfric grinned, and his standard-bearer raised the she-wolf banner high.

"Slaughter, my wolves, slaughter!" screamed Wulfric at the top of his voice.

The Viking army shouted as one in reply, a great cry that rose up to the very sky itself – "Odinnn!"

At the sound of that great pagan roar, the Saxons halted – not out of fear but to redress their line, getting it back into good order after their downhill march. Then they began to advance, giving a great shout of their own. "Hu-oooo!" they bellowed, a low and sonorous sound that went on for many seconds, full of threat and murderous intent. Each time they took a step, the sound of 500 ash-wood spears clashing against iron-rimmed shields filled the air like the footfall of a thousand giants.

The hairs on the back of Corvus' neck began to bristle. The blood began to sing in his veins; the battle-fever was coming upon him.

When the Saxons were some fifty paces from the Viking line, they gave a great roar and charged. The sound of the two armies crashing together was like a thunderclap – surely even the gods in Asgard must have heard them! Spears shivered on iron-bossed shields, axes split wood, helms burst, precious life leaked away into the stony ground.

Corvus' troop was not yet engaged, as no Saxons had yet attempted to take the farm. From the abandoned barn, he had a good view of the battle. The Viking shield wall was dangerously thin, only two deep; the men in the second rank thrust spears over the shoulders of their comrades in front and shoved their shields up against their backs, bracing them in place, pushing against the thrust of the Saxon line. Standing four deep, the Saxons could get a lot more weight behind them, but the low stone wall took away much of their advantage. The *fyrd*men on the flanks were far less effective than the Vikings, but the Huscarls in the centre were a problem. Wulfric was forced to weaken his flanks to bolster his centre; otherwise the Huscarls would have shoved their way through and broken the shield wall. And when a shield wall broke, bloody slaughter followed.

As the sun crossed the sky, the battle continued, stabbing, pushing, shoving. Men died where they stood, and the wall became slippery with blood. The air was filled with the thunder of battle – screaming, shouting and the clash of weapons – but for now, the armies seemed locked in a stalemate. The Saxons could not push past the wall; the Vikings could hold the Saxons back but could not defeat them.

At that moment, Corvus noticed a small knot of men behind the Saxon line, a little way up the sloping foothills of the Suthduns. Banners rippled around a central figure, a greybeard in 'gold-bright splendour' with a crown on his head, mounted on a fine white horse. King Oslac. Beside him stood a tall warrior, resplendent in a fine mail shirt that hung down to his knees, belted at the waist. He leant on a great axe, a shield slung on his back. His helmet was of fine polished steel and a great yellow beard spilled down his chest. Corvus imagined that this must be what Cearl had looked like when he was a young man in his prime.

Behind this small group about fifty *fyrd*men stood in reserve. King Oslac was standing in his stirrups now, scanning the terrain behind the line of battle. Corvus looked back. All he could see was the great forest, and beyond it, the old Roman way and the sweep of more open country-side on the other side of the road. What was Oslac looking at?

The Saxon king gestured, and one of his banner-men dipped his standard. The reserve spearmen began to move around to Oslac's right, heading for the farm. They were going to try and outflank the

Viking line. Corvus pelted down the barn ladder, telling his men to ready themselves. He unhooked his axes from his back and took up position in front of the small shield wall that now covered the most obvious way through the buildings.

At the sight of Corvus in front of a line of hardened Vikings, the Saxons stopped. An officer barked some orders, and they split into two groups, running for the buildings on either side of Corvus' line, evidently preferring their chances in house-to-house fighting to a head-to-head clash of shields. Corvus flicked his axes left and right, and his small shield wall reacted instantly, half one way, half the other, reinforcing their comrades inside the farms and barns. It would be bitter stuff, and they were outnumbered, but they knew they had to hold these buildings. If the Saxons got behind the Viking line, all would be lost.

Corvus considered his options. He could join his men, but he didn't fancy killing a bunch of farmers who were only trying to defend their homes and families from a gang of marauding murderers and thugs. Instead he began to make his way to the front line. Merewyn followed him.

"What are you doing?" she demanded.

"I'm not sure," replied Corvus honestly, hoping he might find a way to further his cause in the chaos of battle.

"What do you mean, you're not sure? What are you up to?" pressed Merewyn.

"I don't know! Now shut up, girl!" said Corvus angrily.

Merewyn narrowed her eyes at that and glared. She didn't like being talked to like that, she didn't like it at all!

But before she could reply, a horn sounded in the direction of the forest. Out of the woods at least fifty Saxon cavalry galloped at high speed. They were behind the Viking line! This was what Oslac had been looking for. They could have been hiding in that wood for days. At the sight of them Merewyn jumped up and down with glee. Corvus was impressed – he had to admire Oslac's strategy. The Saxon cavalry, though small in number, carried long spears and small shields. Their attack on the rear of the Viking line would be devastating. That meant one thing and one thing only...

The Slaughter Wolves were doomed.

CHAPTER 13

WOLF HUNT

It was only a split second before Wulfric spotted the Saxon cavalry charging straight at him and his command unit. He reacted instantly. Stripping fifteen men from the second rank in the centre, he arranged them in front of him, shield to shield, spears bristling, knowing full well no horse would run into a line of spears. But it seemed the Saxons had anticipated this. Instead of closing, they split into two columns and charged to either side of his makeshift shield wall, straight into the backs of the weakened Viking flanks, whose thinner lines were contending with the Saxon *fyrd*men.

Many Vikings died in that first onslaught, defenceless, backs to the foe. Others struggled to defend themselves. Not only that – the centre, where Wulfric had taken the men he needed to form a secondary shield wall, wasn't strong enough now to hold back the powerful Saxon Huscarls. Step by step, the Viking line began to give way. Within moments, the Huscarls were over the wall.

Corvus turned to Merewyn. "Flee," he said. "Flee for your life!"

"Flee?" said Merewyn. "These are my people. I don't need to run from them."

"Trust me," said Corvus. "When the Vikings break – and they will – the Saxons will pursue them. They won't be stopping to ask people whose side they're on. They'll be filled with bloodlust; the slaughter will be indiscriminate and all those on this side of the wall will be fair game."

Merewyn frowned. "I guess you're right. And what about you?" she said.

"I'm going to stick close to Wulfric," said Corvus.

"What, so you can save him again? Protect your blood brother?" said Merewyn witheringly.

"No," Corvus growled, frustration filling him at his inability to convince her of his honesty.

As they were talking, he spotted one of the Slaughter Wolves on the right flank dropping his shield and making a break for it. Another followed close behind.

"Look, there's no time for talk," Corvus went on. "You've got to get away."

"No need. I'll join my fellow slaves. That's the safest place for me. The Saxons will see we're captives, and free us," said Merewyn.

"Yes," said Corvus. "Good idea – that makes sense. Now, go!"

Merewyn looked strangely at Corvus, as if there was something she wanted to say, but thought better of it. She turned away and set off for the Saxon prisoners.

"Good luck, girl," Corvus called after her. "I'm sorry I have to leave you, but if I make it out of this, I'll come find you, I promise, to honour my vow to your father."

"Don't bother." Merewyn looked back at him with hatred in her eyes. "You've already betrayed every oath you ever took!"

Merewyn's words cut Corvus to the bone. What

she said was half true, but it also hurt that Merewyn hated him and thought he was an oath-breaker. But there wasn't time to dwell on her words. The Saxons were breaking through in several places at once, and the Viking line was collapsing. More and more Slaughter Wolves were throwing down their arms and making a run for it. Saxons swept in to left and right, cutting more holes in the line, letting more Saxons through. Corvus ran towards the centre, looking for Wulfric. He could still see the she-wolf banner – but then suddenly it went down under a storm of iron and steel! Out of the confused melee of struggling men, Wulfric suddenly burst forth, like an arrow from the bow, riding for his life. His great black mare was galloping at full pelt – no other horse could match it.

At this, the entire Viking line broke and tried to make a run for it. The Saxons came on after them, just as Corvus had said they would, bloody vengeance in their hearts, pursuing them relentlessly. Everywhere wolf heads were being hunted down and slaughtered.

Corvus sheathed his axes over his back and

dashed after Wulfric as quickly as he could, but the chieftain had already pulled away. As Wulfric drew near to the gaggle of Saxon prisoners, corralled in a rough compound, he changed tack and rode straight through them, slashing with his axe from side to side. Brutally he cut down three of them in seconds.

Corvus was enraged. That was just sheer bloody murder for its own sake, full of spite and malice. He vowed again that he would bring Wulfric down one day, Blood Oath or no Blood Oath!

Then behind him he heard a shout. Riding straight for him was a Saxon horseman, spear levelled. Corvus stopped and turned. As the horseman closed in, Corvus stepped aside deftly, grabbed the spear with both hands and yanked as hard as he could. The Saxon fell from the saddle with a cry, his horse hurtling by without stopping. The Saxon landed well, rolling with the fall, and was up on his feet in a moment, sword drawn. He turned quickly but only in time to receive both of Corvus' thrown axes full in the chest. He went down with a strangled cry. Corvus ran on, pausing only to pluck his axes from their bloody resting place. He neared the Saxon prisoners and spotted Merewyn, safe and well, kneeling by the body of a young man, one of Wulfric's victims. At least she was still alive.

Hearing hoof beats behind him, Corvus turned. There were two of them this time, side by side, heading straight for him. He paused to take aim, and then let loose both axes. Each flew true, and the Saxons crashed to the ground, an axe in each head, a perfect cast. He tried to grab one of the horses as they galloped past, but to no avail, so he dashed back to retrieve his weapons. As he knelt, Slaughter Wolves ran past on either side, dropping weapons, shields and especially wolf-head skins – in the vain hope they might not be recognised. Corvus looked up and saw hundreds of Saxons running straight in his direction! He turned and ran. It had been a mistake to go back; in retrieving his axes, he'd lost valuable seconds. He looked behind to see more horsemen. This was looking bad. He couldn't out-run horsemen. And if he stopped to fight, he'd be overwhelmed by the infantry. The river! It was his only hope.

Changing direction, he pelted hard for the swift-flowing waters, sheathing his axes as he ran. As he reached the bank, he looked behind and saw several Saxons closing in on him. He had to get rid of everything that could weigh him down except for his axes; it would be too dangerous without them. His boots went, as did his shield, leather armour, heavy leather belt and pouch. Diving into the water, axes on his back, he began to swim as fast as he could. The current was strong and in his favour, pulling him further down river. He cast a look behind – a spear splashed into the river nearby and a horseman cantered in after him but soon gave up, the water too deep for his horse. Corvus swam on, cursing under his breath. He'd managed to keep his axes, but once again he had nothing, not even a pair of shoes!

CHAPTER 14

ULFRSHEIM

After a while, the sounds of pursuit faded. He'd escaped. Swimming over to the wooded bank, Corvus hauled himself out of the river, panting with exhaustion. He wanted to rest, but there was no time. Wulfric would have headed back to his settlement, Ulfrsheim, the Wolf's Home. Corvus had to get there too, and find out what was going on. Weary, barefoot, unarmoured, dressed only in a ragged overshirt and trousers, he set off into the woods, at a right angle to the river. At least he still had his battle-brothers slung over his back.

He ought to be able to pick up the trail – any surviving Vikings would head there, and they were bound to leave tracks. The Saxons would soon follow, but they would have stopped to loot the battlefield, tend their wounded and get themselves reorganised after their great victory.

Sure enough, after a short while Corvus came to a trail through the woodland. It was covered with discarded gear, and along the way he found several bodies of Slaughter Wolves who'd died of their wounds before they could make it back to the Viking settlement. Corvus helped himself to a pair of dead man's boots. Luckily they fitted him well, better than his last pair. After a half-hour's walk or so, the trees began to give way, and he emerged from the woods to find himself on a hilltop overlooking a river valley.

The trail led down the hillside to a sturdy stone bridge with a peaked roof of heavy wooden timbers. The river was much bigger and wider than the one he'd just come from, and it flowed east to the sea, some way downstream.

Across the bridge was a large fort, with low stone walls topped by a wooden palisade and several wooden towers placed strategically around the perimeter: so this was it – Ulfrsheim, home of the Slaughter Wolves. Nestled in the bend of the river, about a quarter-mile downstream, was a makeshift harbour with a wooden quay. Moored there was a Viking longship. The fort seemed quiet, as if abandoned, but the longship was a hive of activity. Men were loading it up with supplies. Corvus could make out the head of a she-wolf painted on its great sail. It was Wulfric's ship. Instead of the usual dragon's-head prow, it had a heavy iron ram with massive serrated teeth, ideal for tearing through wood. That iron prow could split an enemy ship in two.

Cautiously, Corvus made his way down to the bridge. As he came down the slope, a figure stood there waiting for him. To his amazement, Corvus realised it was Wulfric's standard-bearer in his ancient armour, a short sword buckled at his belt. The last time Corvus had seen the she-wolf banner, it had gone down under a torrent of Saxon warriors. How had he got out of that alive?

As he walked towards the strange figure, Corvus shook his head in disbelief. There wasn't a mark on the standard-bearer. His faceplate shone in the sun, and his armour didn't even look scratched.

Suddenly, the figure tossed something into the dirt in front of Corvus – his heavy leather belt with its built-in pouch. Corvus had abandoned it at the banks of the river. How had the standard-bearer found it? Corvus picked the belt up, but the buckle was broken, so he slung it around his neck. As he did so, the standard-bearer threw something else at his feet and then simply turned and walked away.

"Wait," shouted Corvus, but the standard-bearer took no notice and walked on. Corvus frowned in puzzlement. A crumpled piece of paper lay at his feet. He picked it up, and a chill went down his spine. It was the note from Ragnar, telling him where Wulfric was and how to kill him. Corvus clapped a hand to his forehead. What an idiot he was! He'd put the note into the leather pouch on his belt. The note that named him, and that revealed all! Wulfric would have read it and worked it all out by now. Why hadn't he destroyed the note when he had the chance?

There was something else, pinned to the top of the note – a brooch. A silver brooch, shaped like a raven with outspread wings. What did it mean?

There was only one way to find out. As Corvus drew nearer to the other side of the bridge, three figures stepped out into the road, blocking his path. The first was Lars Silkbeard, a fresh cut marring the side of his already scarred face. Behind him were two more Slaughter Wolves. One he didn't recognise, but the other was Crop-ears, the grizzled veteran from the Slaughter Wolves' earlier campsite. All three were heavily armed.

"Hello *Corvus*," said Lars, laying a heavy emphasis on his name.

Corvus acknowledged his name with a nod. No point in pretending otherwise now. "What's going on, Lars?" he said.

"Wulfric's leaving in his ship, the *Ironbeard*, heading back to Norway for a time," said Lars. "He can't stay here – not with five hundred Saxons on their way to rip his heart out!" He laughed and spat on the ground before adding, "And you're not coming with us, Corvus."

Corvus digested this. He flicked his eyes over the trio, probing weaknesses; working out a battle plan should it come to blows. They were in full armour, he had none. On the other hand, he was Corvus Gunnarson, and he had two axes.

"What I don't understand..." said Lars. His question tailed off, as if he was unsure whether he should be talking to Corvus at all or simply trying to kill him.

"Yes?" said Corvus.

"Is why didn't you kill Wulfric when you had the chance?" asked Lars. "Why did you save him?"

"It's... complicated," was all Corvus could say.

Crop-ears spoke from behind Lars. "What was that?" he said, his brow furrowed. "Why didn't he kill him?"

"Oh, shut up!" said Lars.

"What?" said Crop-ears.

Lars shook his head and laughed. Corvus couldn't help himself, and a smile appeared at the corner of his mouth as well.

"You know, Corvus, this whole thing is a shame, really – I rather liked you," said Lars.

"Are we going to kill him now?" said the third Viking in a loud, booming voice. He was a big, hairy bear of a man with arms like tree trunks. Corvus assessed him. He was strong – no doubt he could wield that great axe as if it were a walking stick – but he'd be slow, easy to hit.

"We're not supposed to," said Crop-ears.

Corvus looked at Lars inquiringly.

Lars nodded. "It's true. Wulfric said you can live, go free if you want, because you saved his life. If you walk away, he'll spare you. If you come after him, he'll hunt you down, blood brother or not. He may have lost most of his men today, but he has more back home. As soon as the three of us board, we'll be leaving, and Wulfric will be back with another army next year. Bigger. Better. And then Oslac will pay. Walk away now, and you won't have to worry about Wulfric."

"It's not me who needs to worry," said Corvus.

Lars looked at him uncomprehendingly, as if he were mad. "By the eye of Odin, Corvus, it's Wulfric you're talking about! Men like him always get what they want. He's ruthless, powerful, rich. Walk away, man, while you still can!" he said, with a half-smile.

"Were you at the 'Gunnarson House Party',

Lars?" Corvus asked suddenly.

The smile faded from Lars' lips, and his face went blank, like stone, mute and expressionless. He lifted his sword defensively, changed his stance, but said nothing. That was answer enough for Corvus. He'd been there, no doubt about it. Lars raised his head, looked up at the sky and sighed.

Corvus seized the moment. He reached for his battle-brothers, drew them forth with practised speed and hurled them with all his might. One flew to the right of Lars and split Crop-ears' face in two, killing him instantly. One flew to the left and bit deep into the other man's neck. He dropped his axe and with a hideous, gurgling sound sank to his knees, scrabbling at his mangled throat.

Lars' face took on an almost comical look of amazement. One of his companions was dead, the other dying, their lifeblood wasting away on the dusty track, all in the blink of an eye. Corvus just stood there, blue eyes blazing under a crown of raven-black hair. Lars went pale. Then he gave an inarticulate roar and charged, sword raised to strike, shield up front.

Corvus whipped the heavy leather belt from behind his neck, blocking Lars' sword with it. Then he twisted it around the shaft of the blade and dived into a forward roll, dragging the sword out of Lars' grip. As he came up on his feet, he had his belt in one hand, sword in the other.

Lars stood there, frozen in shocked disbelief. In a matter of seconds his companions were dead, and he'd been robbed of his weapon.

"What now, Lars?" said Corvus, his voice tight with anger. "Not so easy as an old man and his wife, eh? My father. My mother."

Lars took a step back. He hurled his shield at Corvus, then turned and ran. Corvus ducked, then threw the sword point-first at Lars' fleeing form. The sword smashed straight through his back and out the other side. Lars fell forward on to his knees, gasping. Corvus walked over and stood in front of him. Lars was staring down at the gore-stained blade sticking out of his chest.

"Incredible," he said, coughing blood.

"What happened to my sisters?" growled Corvus.

"Ah, well," Lars coughed. "That would be... unh, that would be telling!"

"*Tell me*!" said Corvus, gripping Lars by the neck.

Lars looked up at Corvus. A ghost of a smile played around his mouth. "Wulfric gave them away..." he croaked.

"Gave them? To who?" demanded Corvus.

"To Oslac. King of the Saxons. He still owed him final payment... part of the deal for the land where we built the fort, here by the river," he sputtered weakly. "The Saxons call it the Tamesis... nice bit of land."

His voice tailed off. He gave a last cough of blood, and fell forward, dead, his well-groomed, silken beard now mired in blood and gore.

Corvus stared at the body for a moment or two. Oslac, the Saxon king. How ironic. Well, that was that, then. He'd have to stay here. He had to get his sisters back, before he could even think about going after Wulfric. Cleaning and sheathing his axes, he walked over to the side of the bridge, shaking his head at this latest turn of events.

Below, Wulfric's longship, the *Ironbeard*, set off down the river, oars rippling in the afternoon sun. At the back of the ship stood Wulfric's strange lieutenant, banner in hand, looking back at him enigmatically. Corvus took out the raven brooch and examined it once more. What did it mean? What was the standard-bearer trying to tell him?

Corvus watched as Wulfric made his escape. After a while, he turned and walked back up to the fort. Its gates lay open, its towers untended. It was empty. Corvus managed to scavenge some scraps of food. Once he'd eaten, he went to the front of fort, and sat down to watch for King Oslac and his army, but exhaustion took him, and he fell into a deep sleep. He dreamt of his mother and father. His father smiling broadly, his mother looking worried, a sad, hurt look in her eyes. Then he dreamt of a raven, perched on the tombstones of his parents, cawing into the desolate sky like an omen of death and despair.

CHAPTER 15

OSLAC, KING OF THE SAXONS

*C*orvus woke with a start, dreams of burning homesteads and ravens fading from his mind. It was early evening and the tramp of booted feet, the jangle of war-gear and the rattle of spears had woken him. Trooping down the slope towards the bridge was Oslac's Saxon army. At its head was the king.

Corvus cursed himself for falling asleep. Running forward, he took up a position on his side of the bridge and waited.

After a time, the vanguard approached and came to a halt on the other side of the bridge. Behind them the Saxon army drew itself up. There was a pause. The bridge was narrow, no more than three men wide. A skilled warrior could hold it for some time on his own. And, to the Saxons, Corvus looked like a skilled warrior.

King Oslac sat on a great white horse, flanked by two other mounted nobles, with several captains nearby on foot. The king was the wrong side of middle-aged, with a long grey beard and a wrinkled face. He looked like a man who had seen much. His eyes were rheumy and yellowing around the edges but still held a keen light, a piercing intelligence.

One of the men standing next to the king was the golden-bearded warrior Corvus had noticed at the battle, the one who had reminded him of Cearl. He wore fine armour, and the visor of his helm was up. He had a wide-open, honest face and a build similar to Corvus' own. He looked like he knew how to handle himself.

One of the king's men spoke. "Who are you? Where is Wulfric?"

"Wulfric has fled in his ship with his remaining men. I am Corvus Gunnarson," said Corvus.

"We are too late, then, Sighere, the bird has

flown," said the king to the man mounted on a horse beside him.

"Yes, Uncle, as we expected," said Sighere, a dark-eyed, prematurely bald young man. He turned back to Corvus and said, "You are a Viking, are you not?"

"I am," said Corvus.

Sighere's face became a mask of hatred. "A Viking Slaughter Wolf! Do you have some message from your master, then, before you die?"

"I am no Slaughter Wolf!" said Corvus. "In fact, I fought with Cearl against the Slaughter Wolves."

The golden-bearded warrior frowned. "There was talk of a great Viking warrior who sided with the men of Wotanhirst," he said.

"Pah!" said Sighere with venom. "They're all the same, Viking scum!"

"I may be scum, but at least I'm not bald," quipped Corvus without thinking.

Immediately he regretted it. Sighere went puce with anger, and when one or two Saxons chuckled, he got even angrier.

"You'll die for that, you worm, you lice-ridden

dog, you..." he shouted, spittle flying from his lips.

The king put up a hand to silence his nephew. Sighere glared angrily, bridling at the king's command. Resentfully, he fell silent.

"What is it you do here, then, Corvus Gunnarson," the king said, "other than insult us while you are outnumbered? Five hundred to one, in fact," he added.

"Forgive me, lord," said Corvus. "I am but a simple soldier. All I have is a question for you, great king."

The king raised an eyebrow. "What is that to us? We have other matters to attend to."

"I am no friend of Wulfric's," said Corvus, "In fact, I would like nothing better than to see him dead. He killed my..."

"THAT'S A LIE!" shouted a voice from behind the king.

A young woman raced forward from the ranks of the Saxon army, thin and hollow-cheeked, her long, brown hair tied in a ponytail. Corvus' heart sank. It was Merewyn.

"Don't do it, girl!" shouted Corvus.

The king and his men turned in surprise. This

was getting interesting.

"He is a friend of Wulfric's. More than that, he is Wulfric's blood brother. He saved his life!" cried Merewyn at the top of her voice, pointing accusingly at Corvus.

All eyes swung back to Corvus. "Is this true?" said the king.

"Well, er, technically," said Corvus, flicking his eyes behind him, judging whether or not he could make a run for it. This wasn't going well. The king narrowed his eyes.

"Kill this Viking dog!" said Sighere, waving up some Huscarls. The golden-bearded warrior, Cearl's lookalike, glanced at the king. The Huscarls paused, waiting to see if the order would be countermanded. The king said nothing.

"Wait!" said Corvus loudly. "I challenge you! I challenge the king!" The golden-bearded warrior frowned. The king raised an eyebrow.

Sighere snorted, dismissing his words as absurdity. Behind him, soldiers unhooked shields from their backs, took up spears and swords.

"Under the ancient rules of honour duels!"

said Corvus.

"The king is an old man; you are ridiculous!" said Sighere. Twenty Saxon Huscarls marched towards the bridge.

"But he has a champion, does he not? That is honourable, a champion's duel!" said Corvus desperately. Why, oh why, had he insulted Sighere? Why couldn't he control his tongue?

The soldiers began preparing for a charge, three men at the front, shields at the fore, more men behind them, ready to thrust spearheads over their shoulders.

"If I lose, then you have another Viking notch on your belt of victory. If I win, all I ask is that the king answer one question!" Corvus shouted.

The Huscarls paused, waiting for the final order from the king. The golden-bearded warrior put his hand on the king's bridle and said, "It's a fair challenge, my lord."

Sighere growled. "Shut up, Edric!" he said to the golden warrior.

The king sighed. "Oh, just cut him down," he said. Sighere smirked in triumph. The Huscarls shifted uneasily.

"Wait! I will fight him!" said Edric, the golden-bearded warrior. "Sire, I am your champion, give me this honour, I beg you!"

The Huscarls cheered. The Saxons in front began to chant, "Edric! Edric! Edric!"

The king raised his eyes to heaven. He was older, wiser. To him these young fools fighting for glory were just that – young fools. But now his warriors were fired up, so he had little choice but to let it go ahead or risk resentment and unpopularity.

"So be it," he said. "My champion, Edric, will fight Corvus in single combat! Prepare the duelling ground!"

Corvus sighed in relief. Once more he'd bought himself another roll of the dice in his great game of chance with the Grim Reaper.

But Sighere's face darkened. He spat and muttered a curse under his breath. Then he hissed, "You'd better gut the stinking swine, Edric, or – "

The king cut him short with a wave of the hand. Sighere glowered resentfully once more but fell silent under his command.

CHAPTER 16

DUEL OF CHAMPIONS

Corvus backed away from the bridge into the open ground in front of the fort. A large duelling circle was formed, made up of a ring of a hundred or so Saxon Huscarls. An ornate wooden chair was brought forward for King Oslac, who sat, flanked by his captains and his nephew, Earl Sighere the Bald. The earl turned and beckoned someone over. Merewyn appeared, excitement and uncertainty on her face. Sighere gestured for her to sit at his feet.

Corvus stood waiting, armoured in the old leather he had taken from Wulfric's fort but without a shield, twin axes slung on his back. Edric entered the ring covered in full mail, sword at his belt, shield on one arm and spear in the other. His shield was brightly painted with a golden dragon, or wyvern, on a red background.

He paused. "Don't you want a shield? Some other weapons? A helmet perhaps?" he asked.

"No, this is fine," said Corvus.

Edric frowned. "Wait," he said, and walked out of the ring. The audience sighed, wanting the show to start.

After a few minutes, Edric returned. He'd removed his helmet and taken off his mail, replacing it with borrowed leathers, the same as Corvus. He was also shieldless, now armed with a long spear in both hands and a sword at his belt.

"Let it not be said that Edric takes unfair advantage," he declaimed to the assembled warriors, who cheered loudly. When the cheering faded, Edric turned to Corvus and sank into a half-crouch, two-handed spear pointed unerringly at Corvus' throat.

Corvus drew forth his axes with a snappy flourish. Then he and Edric began circling each other.

Slowly they wheeled around, each sizing the other up, looking for an opening, an opportunity to strike. Edric's spear had a longer reach, but if Corvus could get in under its shaft, he'd have the advantage of two deadly close-quarter weapons.

Corvus thought about throwing one of his axes. But Edric looked fast and agile, well able to dodge.

While Corvus was still considering his next move, Edric suddenly jabbed his spear at Corvus' face with whiplike speed. Corvus leapt back smartly. But instead of pulling the spear back, Edric drove it into the ground, and then vaulted into the air, driving both of his feet straight at Corvus' chest!

Corvus was taken completely by surprise – he'd never seen a move like that before. At the last moment he managed to dive aside, hitting the ground shoulder-first, rolling and then bouncing nimbly back to his feet. The crowd gave a roar of appreciation as the combatants began circling once more. Corvus had been caught off guard, but he'd be ready next time. Let Edric try that one again – he'd cut both his feet off at the ankles.

Suddenly Edric thrust the spear at Corvus' legs. Corvus parried with one axe and cut down at Edric's head with the other. Edric parried the blow with the back end of his spear. There followed a flurry of cuts, thrusts, hacks and parries of mind-numbing speed, accompanied by the clang and thud of wood and iron. The crowd sat enthralled, amazed. After a few moments there was a single short cry, and both men stepped back, panting.

A trickle of blood welled up and ran down Corvus' cheek. Edric's spear point had gouged a line across the side of his face. The crowd roared its approval. Edric had won the first round.

Corvus narrowed his eyes. He'd been over-confident. He'd never met anyone this skilled with the spear. In fact, he'd never met anyone he couldn't beat in a fight. Edric was as fast and as strong as Corvus. Could it really be possible that he had met his match? Corvus wiped the blood off his face. Absent-mindedly he licked the blood from his fingers, staring at Edric, calculating options. He had to neutralise that spear. Disarm him or break it somehow.

Without warning, Edric began to whirl the spear in the air, round and round over his head. He advanced slowly, step by step. Corvus was forced to give ground, ducking, dodging, searching for an opening. Then he saw his chance. Stepping in, he blocked the whirling spear with one axe, lashing out with the other, straight at the side of Edric's head. But Edric had been anticipating this. Dropping into a crouch, he brought the butt end of the spear around in an arc, knocking Corvus' legs out from under him.

Corvus went down hard on his back. A split second later and Edric was above him, driving the spear at his chest. It was only Corvus' lightning reflexes that saved him. He managed to roll aside just in time, so that the spearhead caught only the edge of his leather breastplate, skittering off into the earth. For a moment, Edric's spear was caught, buried in the ground – Corvus twisted up on to one knee and whipped both axes across, cutting the spear in two, leaving the spearhead and three feet of wooden haft sticking up out of the ground, and three feet of wood in Edric's hands. Without a second's thought, Edric brought the wooden shaft hard down on the back of Corvus' wrists, knocking both axes out of his hands, and then brought it sharply back and up, cracking Corvus across the side of his head and sending him flying backwards to lie in the dirt on his back once more, stunned.

Another great cry went up from the crowd. Corvus leapt to his feet, just in time to dodge the wooden shaft Edric had hurled at him. Edric drew his sword. Corvus had nothing. This was bad.

Without hesitation Edric came in, slashing at Corvus, who dived and rolled away, coming up with the wooden shaft in his hand, Edric was hot on his heels, cutting at him once more. Corvus turned the blade away with the wooden shaft, careful not to let the sword blade split the wood. He parried another cut, and then dodged aside, twisting, trying to reach his axes, but Edric managed to get between him and his goal.

There was a pause. It was obvious that Edric wasn't nearly as good with the sword as he was with the spear.

"Finish him, you fool!" shouted Sighere. "He's only got a bit of old wood!"

Edric frowned, then darted forward, lunging with the sword. Corvus sidestepped, but Edric brought the sword around, slashing at his head. Corvus ducked and shoved the wooden shaft between Edric's ankles. Edric lost his footing and stumbled forward. That was all the time Corvus needed. Diving for his axes, he came up to face Edric with one in each hand.

Another roar from the crowd.

Corvus paced forward, striking with his axes: an overhead cut, a cut to the side of the head, down to the legs in a rapid blur of ever-changing attacks. Edric had to give ground, desperately blocking as best he could. He only had the one weapon, whereas Corvus had two, which he could wield just as well as – in fact better than – any man with one. Edric grunted – an axe head had nicked his arm. Then he grimaced – a barely parried axe had opened a cut over his eyes. Blood ran down, obscuring his vision.

The crowd went quiet. Corvus crouched, hooked

an axe head around the back of Edric's ankle and then straightened fast, driving his shoulder full into Edric's chest. Edric went down on to his back with a crash, arms and legs splayed. In an instant, Corvus was over him, one booted foot pinning his sword hand to the ground. He brought an axe down into the earth, an inch from Edric's head, and raised the other high.

"Yield!" Corvus shouted, "Yield!"

Edric, half blinded by blood, struggled for a second, trying to free his sword hand.

Corvus raised his axe to strike. "Don't do it," he hissed. "You don't have to die."

Edric looked up at Corvus. Their eyes locked. Then he sank back, knowing he was beaten. "I yield," he said.

The crowd gave a collective groan. Merewyn looked on, her face a mask, as if she didn't know whether to be glad Corvus had won or sorry that he hadn't been killed.

Corvus stepped back. He offered a hand to Edric, who looked up at him resentfully. Then he sighed, and took Corvus' hand. Corvus heaved him to his feet.

"Never have I seen such skill with the spear. That was the closest fight I've ever had," said Corvus, taking in great gulps of air. He was exhausted.

"And mine," replied Edric, wiping the blood from his eyes.

"You could have won that easily, if you'd kept your helmet, shield and mail shirt and taken a second spear instead of that sword," said Corvus between breaths.

"Aye, but that wouldn't have been fair, would it?" said Edric.

"Most men wouldn't risk their lives in the name of fairness. It was a noble gesture. I will never forget it," said Corvus gravely, placing a hand on Edric's shoulder.

They looked at each other. Edric pointed at the deep cut on the side of Corvus' head, still dripping with blood.

"That'll scar up nicely. It'll remind you of me every time you look in a mirror," he said.

Corvus laughed, pointing at the cut over Edric's eye. "And that one will remind you of me!"

"Not as bad as yours, though," Edric replied. Corvus burst out laughing, slapping Edric on the back. They grinned at each other.

Corvus turned to the king and raised his axes high in a gesture of victory. Oslac acknowledged him with a nod. Sighere spat.

Corvus slung his axes and leant on his knees, panting. Edric walked back to stand with the king. Oslac looked up at him, slapped a hand on his back. "You fought well, my champion," he said.

"Pah, he's a fool," muttered Sighere. "Giving up your best gear in the name of honour! Idiot!"

The king silenced him with a wave of his hand.

"It was a good fight," said the king. Turning to Corvus, he added, "And I am grateful that you spared Edric, our champion. What is your question?"

"Wulfric murdered my parents," said Corvus, still panting, "and took my sisters, Freia and Ingrid." He could see Merewyn looking at him, a frown of puzzlement on her face. Corvus paused to get more breath.

"His crimes are legion," said Oslac. "What of it?"

Corvus went on. "I have been trying to find out what happened to my sisters. This morning I learnt that Wulfric gifted them to you, King Oslac, as slaves," he said.

Sighere raised an eyebrow at that.

"I see," said the king. "It is true that we did receive tribute from Wulfric, before he betrayed us. Among them were many slaves."

"If you could tell me where they are, my lord, perhaps even allow me to purchase them from you, or perform some service in return for their freedom," said Corvus.

"Perhaps," said Oslac, "though I do not know where they are now. I cannot be expected to remember every slave that comes to my court, can I?"

Edric leant forward and whispered something in the king's ear. Sighere strained to hear, scowling with irritation.

The king said, "You will accompany us back to our capital, Selsea. There we will make inquiries as to the fate of your sisters. Then perhaps we can come to some kind of arrangement." With that he stood up and addressed his troops.

"We camp in Ulfrsheim tonight! We shall make that well-built fort our own and leave a garrison there. From this day forward it will be named Ulfrsheim no more, but 'Kingstown-on-Tamesis'. Tomorrow we march for home!"

CHAPTER 17

THE KING'S HALL

Corvus strode through the main street of Selsea towards the king's hall. Two Saxon Huscarls accompanied him. He'd been summoned to the king's court at last.

A week had passed since his duel with Edric. He had marched with Oslac's army back to the Saxon capital almost as a prisoner, technically free, but with the two Huscarls at his side the entire time. Sighere had assigned them to him. "Keep an eye on that Viking dog," he'd said. Sighere was going to be a problem; Corvus could feel it in his bones.

During the trip he hadn't seen or heard from Merewyn or Edric, nor had he heard from them since. When they'd arrived at Selsea, a large walled city, teeming with people, Corvus had been billeted with his Huscarl guards in a simple wooden barracks near the town gate and told to wait until the king sent for him. That was three days ago.

Selsea was a large settlement, built on a peninsula and virtually cut off from the mainland. Its walls went back to Roman times, but it had been extensively rebuilt since then, though in wood instead of stone. It was easy to defend. Anyone trying to reach it by land had to cross a single bridge or take the ferry. The only other way to get to the city was by sea, and Selsea had extensive docks. In the centre of the town was the king's hall, where Corvus was going now.

He'd been expecting something similar to Cearl's hall, but this was far more impressive. Originally a Roman civic building, its front was made up of four great marble pillars and a peaked roof with carvings – a frieze depicting a long-forgotten battle. The rest of it had stone foundations upon which the Saxons had erected an imposing timber hall of great size. Huscarls stood on guard beneath the marble columns, looking impressive in full-face helms and gleaming mail shirts. Legs apart, they stood with both hands resting on the heads of their great axes.

As they reached the front of the building, Corvus noticed the doors: massive, tall and black, and covered in iron bosses. As he drew near, he realised the doors were actually made of iron as well. Probably the original doors, he thought to himself, for it was well known that the Romans built like gods, as if for giants. His companions opened the huge doors; they had to lean on them, pushing hard with their shoulders. Slowly the great edifice creaked open, and Corvus and his guards walked into the cool gloom of Oslac's hall, where the stone façade gave way to good Saxon timber. The hall was high and long, lit by sunlight from chimney holes in the wooden roof. Smoke curled up from several fireplaces, where meat was being cooked, fish smoked and bread baked.

Corvus strode down a long walkway, flanked by wooden pillars that rose up to the high roof. The wood was carved and painted – mostly with stories and tales from the life of the White Christ. Overhead he spotted a large jagged hole in the roof, caused by a storm, perhaps, or just wear and tear. A long ladder ran up to the hole, and at the top, he could see a workman inspecting the damage. The floor of the walkway was paved with old Roman flagstones, some with interlaid mosaic patterns. On either side, people worked in the shadows – cooking, weaving, making armour and weapons. Corvus could see a blacksmith, and next to him, a small mint, where a man worked striking gold and silver coins with Oslac's seal on them.

Ahead was a stepped dais with a large stone throne on top, inlaid with alabaster, gold and silver. And there sat Oslac, a ceremonial spear and shield propped up on either side of him. The spearhead was solid gold. The shield was richly painted, and its boss was solid silver. On Oslac's left stood his champion, Edric, on a lower step of the dais. On his right was Earl Sighere the Bald, his nephew and heir to the throne of Sussex, carefully making sure he was standing on a higher step than Edric, of course. A little in front of the throne was a wizened old priest with a staff, no doubt the royal chamberlain. Arranged on either side of an audience space were various advisors, captains, nobles and other members of Oslac's court.

Corvus gulped. He wasn't used to this kind of formal audience. Seeing Corvus, Edric nodded and gave him a friendly smile, to which Corvus gave him a half smile in return. Ruefully he noticed that the cut above Edric's eye had healed up well. It would leave a scar, but nothing compared to the one Corvus would have on his cheek from Edric's gouging spear.

"Greetings, Corvus Gunnarson," said Oslac. "You may approach." The wizened old priest beckoned him forward.

Corvus walked up to the dais and stood before the king. Oslac raised an eyebrow. The little old priest reached up and slapped Corvus on the shoulder. "Down," he hissed.

"What?" said Corvus.

"On one knee, you great lummox," said the priest.

"Oh, I see! Sorry," said Corvus. He dropped to one knee and looked up.

"Bow your head until you're asked to speak,

you fat ox, you dunderheaded barbarian!" said the priest, his cracked old voice rising to a shriek.

Corvus lowered his head, muttering under his breath, "All right, all right, no need to go on about it."

On the dais, Edric stifled a laugh. Even the king's mouth twitched a little. Then Oslac spoke.

"Welcome to our court, Corvus. We have made inquiries as to your sisters' fate, and we have had some success."

Corvus looked up expectantly. The chamberlain slapped him on the top of his head, so Corvus bowed it again.

"Your sisters are nearby. They are working as cloth-makers, weaving flax grown on our royal farms. They have been treated well and are unharmed. Indeed, they are skilled weavers, valued highly by the guildmaster. For that reason, some of us are reluctant to give them up." Oslac glanced at Sighere.

He went on. "However, Edric Godwyn, my champion, has interceded on your behalf. We can release your sisters to you, in exchange for a task we would have you perform for us."

"Name it, lord!" said Corvus, barely able to keep the excitement out of his voice.

"Of late, our pastures, teeming with sheep, have been under attack. Once more we are threatened by wolves – but these are not the two-legged kind from the north. Those we have dealt with already."

"Not quite all of them, though," muttered Sighere under his breath, staring pointedly at Corvus. The king pretended not to hear, and went on.

"No, these are four-legged wolves – but of a kind none of us have ever seen before, not since the days of legend when the war god Tiw fought the Fenris wolf. These are vicious, and they have attacked our flocks relentlessly. Hunt this pack down. Destroy them. In return we shall hand back your sisters to you."

A puzzled frown appeared on Corvus' face. "You may speak," said the king.

Corvus looked up, glancing gingerly at the old priest, as if expecting another flurry of slaps. None came. "Is that all, lord? All I have to do is hunt down and kill some wolves?" he said.

The king replied, "Hah! By Wotan's arse, don't think for a second that I'm doing you a favour, son," he said, forgetting his formal court speech for a moment.

A pained expression appeared on the chamberlain's face. "My lord! Need I remind you that the church does not look favourably on such language? The old gods like Tiw and Wotan are nothing but devils and demons sent by Satan himself to tempt men aside from the True Faith. It is not seemly for you..."

"All right, all right, I'll pray for forgiveness later," interrupted Oslac in an irritated tone. He sighed and continued, falling back into the language of the court.

"Be assured – these wolves are not like other wolves. They are man-killers, unusually large and cunning. Already we have lost many sheep and cattle, and several farmers, too. Two groups of skilled hunters, the second led by my chief wolf-catcher, are lost, presumed dead. No, it is no easy task. Therefore we will send with you Edric, our champion. We will also send two hunters, the brothers

Aldfrid and Aldhelm, who have in turn been sent to aid us by the high king, Offa of Mercia. Also Merewyn of Wotanhirst, who has asked to go with you. She is a skilled hunter and tracker. Do you agree to this?"

"I do, lord," said Corvus. Merewyn? What was in her mind? Either way, it would be a good opportunity to try and square things with her.

"Good. You may go now – Edric will arrange the details with you. I am placing him in charge of the expedition."

The priest coughed expectantly. Oslac raised his eyes. "May the blessings of Christ go with you," he added.

Corvus got to his feet and turned to leave. This drew another flurry of slaps from the priest, "No, fool! Backwards, bowing – no man turns his back on the king!"

Corvus grunted in irritation, but he did as he was told, shuffling backwards, bowing the whole time. The king watched him go, hand over his mouth, eyes dancing, trying not to laugh. Sighere, however, eyed Corvus with barely concealed hatred.

CHAPTER 18

THE FOREST OF ANDRED

The rest of the day was spent equipping their expedition. Edric put together a week's worth of rations (dried meat, fish, cheese and bread), hunting spears, bows, arrows and various other useful pieces of equipment. Edric, Corvus and Merewyn would carry most of the gear in leather backpacks. The two Mercian brothers, Aldfrid and Aldhelm, would travel light, for they would act as the expedition's scouts and trackers. Edric said the wolf pack had struck recently, killing ten sheep on a farmer's land a day to the east of Selsea. The Mercian brothers, a pair of taciturn hunters, recommended they track the wolves from there. Edric agreed.

The next morning they set off early, the Mercian brothers ranging ahead, Edric, Corvus and Merewyn marching along behind. An uncomfortable silence fell on the trio. Neither Merewyn nor Corvus would look at the other.

After a while, Edric called a halt. "This cannot go on," he said. "We may be going into great danger, and we will have to be united, sure of purpose. We can't have trouble in the ranks."

Merewyn glanced at Corvus. Edric went on. "Whatever it is that is between you, it must be resolved. Now!"

Corvus sighed. He was right, this couldn't go on, so he came to a stop. Merewyn pulled up too, rather more abruptly. Taking Edric's words as her cue, she put her hands on her hips, turned to face Corvus and let him have a piece of her mind.

"Why did you save Wulfric's life, you traitor?" she said angrily. "He was responsible for my father's death. And then you let them enslave me, after you swore an oath to my father to protect me, as he lay dying! A death oath, for Jesus' sake!"

Edric raised an eyebrow. Corvus looked down.

"Well," he began.

But Merewyn wasn't finished. "And then, to cap it all, you joined his war band! You told me you'd sworn an oath of vengeance against Wulfric, that you'd sworn to kill him. But instead of killing Wulfric, you killed the man who was about to kill him. And then, worst of all, you became his blood brother! Why?"

"Well," Corvus repeated, "I..."

Merewyn rushed on, the words pouring out of her. "And yet you fought like a demon against Wulfric's men at Wotanhirst. I thought you'd fight to the death – I was going to die by your side. Then at that big battle, you helped me escape. You said you thought the Saxons deserved to win, that they had right on their side. You didn't warn Wulfric about the Saxon cavalry when you could have. It doesn't make any sense." The words dried up. She'd finished.

Edric looked over at Corvus. This was going to be interesting.

Corvus had been thinking about what to say to Merewyn for quite a while.

"It was all because of my sisters." Corvus' words spilled out.

"Go on," she said.

"I knew Wulfric had taken them, but I didn't know where they were. And I couldn't very well ask someone, could I? I had to pretend to be someone else, infiltrate Wulfric's band. Once I knew where my sisters were, I could kill Wulfric – but not until then. As far as I knew, he was the only one who knew their fate. So I ended up saving him.

"After I killed Ragnar," he went on, "Wulfric made me his blood brother, much to my disgust, and now whatever I do I will be an oath-breaker. If I let him live, I break my vow of vengeance. If I kill him, I break my Blood Oath. As for your enslavement – what else could I do? It was slavery or death, so that was the best way I could keep my oath to your father.

"But now I know where my sisters are," Corvus continued. "Before I killed him, Lars Silkbeard told me that Wulfric had given them to King Oslac. So Wulfric will die, Blood Oath or not."

Merewyn looked up. "You killed Lars Silkbeard,

one of Wulfric's captains?" she said.

"Aye, said Corvus, "He was with Wulfric when they murdered my parents, so he deserved it."

"Ah," said Edric, "that would explain the three Vikings we found dead on the bridge at Ulfrsheim – or Kingstown-on-Tamesis, as it is called now."

Merewyn frowned. "Your sisters. I see." She fell silent, deep in thought. Corvus stared at her for a moment, but it was obvious the conversation was over for now. After a few seconds, Edric came to the same conclusion and said, "Well, let's hope that's cleared the air, then. On we go."

Later in the day, the Mercian brothers joined them on the trail. They had picked up wolf tracks from the farm, and had followed them across country. By early evening the party had reached the outskirts of the Forest of Andred, a huge forest that ran across most of Sussex. By nightfall they had penetrated a few miles into the forest. They stopped under a great oak and made camp.

As they sat around a fire, staring into the flames, Merewyn suddenly spoke. "I'm sorry, Corvus. I misjudged you."

Corvus shrugged. "It's all right. I can see why."

"Will you forgive me?" she said.

"Of course. Forget about it," said Corvus. "Actually, I learnt a great lesson that day, a lesson in humility. That I am not the best warrior that has ever lived, that I can be beaten." He looked over at Edric. "And I also made a new friend. Even though he has left me scarred for life!"

At that, Edric laughed, raising a hand to the scar over his eyebrow. "And I, too – though not nearly as badly as you!" he said.

Corvus grinned. "So, Merewyn, I should thank you for that – you did me a favour."

Merewyn lay back with a sigh of relief. There was little more to be said, so they set watches and went to sleep.

The next day was much like the first, threading their way through deep forest, the Mercian brothers leading the way, the others following along behind, feeling useless. Merewyn was a good tracker, but compared with the Mercian brothers she was an amateur. Edric knew only the arts of war and courtly ways, and Corvus could hunt a little and fight, but like most Vikings, he was a much better seaman than he was a tracker.

After an uneventful day, where, save for the birds, they neither saw nor even heard a single animal, let alone a wolf, they found a crumbling ruin of some ancient stone, overgrown and long ago eaten up by the forest. Here they set up camp for another night.

They ate sparingly of their rations, sitting around the fire near the ruins. Edric watched the Mercian brothers, who sat a little apart, looking troubled and talking in what for them was an animated way. Edric walked over to them. As he approached, they fell silent.

"What's the problem, lads?" asked Edric.

The brothers exchanged looks. "It's the tracks," said one. Corvus thought it was Aldfrid, but he couldn't be sure. The brothers were difficult to tell apart, and they barely spoke.

"The tracks – what about them?" prompted Edric.

"They're not right," said the other brother.

"What do you mean, 'they're not right'?" asked Edric. "Come on, spit it out, don't make me drag it out of you!"

The brothers looked at each other, as if deciding who would speak.

"It's almost as if they were put there on purpose," said one.

"To lead us in," said the other.

"What – like a trap or something?" said Edric. "But they're only wolves, by the blood of Christ! How could that be?"

The brothers shrugged. "Indeed," said one.

"How could that be?" said the other. They fell into silence, their dark eyes glinting in the firelight.

"Well, what do you think we should do about it?" said Edric.

One of them shrugged. "Don't know," said the other.

Edric sighed in frustration. "Well, we'll just have to go on," he said. "They are only wolves. And we have bows, and spears and axes. And Corvus Gunnarson, one of the greatest warriors I have ever seen."

The brothers nodded in agreement but said

nothing more. Edric tramped back to the fire and sat down. Corvus frowned. If those two, said to be the best hunters and trackers in the kingdom of Mercia, were spooked... well, that didn't bode well.

They stared into the flames, each wrapped up in their own thoughts. Corvus gazed at the raven brooch the standard-bearer had given him. The exquisite silver workmanship glinted in the firelight. Somehow it seemed familiar to Corvus. What did it mean?

Meanwhile, the Mercian brothers stood watch, silent, enigmatic, as if they were part of the forest itself.

CHAPTER 19

BERSERKER-WOLF

The following morning was hot, very hot. The brothers left to scout ahead, whilst the others walked through the forest, which was filled with a stifling heat. Insects buzzed around them, hoping for an easy meal – already they itched from several bites. By noon, one of the brothers came back to find them.

"We've found something," he said, in an almost excited tone. "A hollow in the forest."

"A hollow?" said Edric.

"Yes, like a bowl. Maybe thirty feet in diameter. With what might be a cave mouth down below, to one side. It may be their lair. It's about two hundred yards that way," he said, pointing north.

"We'd better get up there, then," said Corvus.

"No, not yet," said the hunter. "Stay here, make no noise. We'll scout the hollow first, see if they're really there, work out the best line of attack. We should be able to flush them straight into your arms, so you can dispatch them."

It made sense, so Edric nodded his agreement. "All right, then, we'll wait. Good luck!"

The hunter acknowledged his words with a half-smile, before turning and soundlessly disappearing into the trees like a ghost.

"Was that a smile?" said Merewyn.

"You know, I think it was," said Edric.

"And a veritable saga of words, by their standards," said Corvus with a chuckle.

All three of them felt a great sense of relief, looking forward to some action after all that trudging through the forest, fighting off the midges and gnats in the perpetual gloom of thick woodland.

They settled down to wait. And waited. Gnats and midges assaulted them in huge numbers. After an hour, Corvus began to get worried, though Merewyn pointed out that silent tracking and scouting could be very time-consuming.

After two hours, Corvus couldn't stand it any more.

"We have to go after them," he said. "Something has gone wrong. Anyway, I can't take another insect bite." The other two had to agree. It had been too long. They moved forward, trying to be silent, but only Merewyn could manage it as well as the brothers. The other two simply didn't have the woodcraft, so they abandoned any attempt at silence and started forward at a quick but noisy trot. After a few minutes they came to a woodland track, made by the passage of animals over many years. They followed it to the brim of a wide bowl, a depression in the forest floor. The track ran down through wild undergrowth.

They paused at the top. Edric shouted at the top of his voice, "Aldfrid! Aldhelm! Where are you?"

The forest had fallen silent. Animal sounds stopped. Birds ceased to sing in the trees. Only the creak of ancient timbers and the soughing of leaves in the faint breeze answered Edric's call.

He shouted again. Nothing. Even the silence was

stifling. Merewyn frowned. "What?" whispered Corvus, intimidated by the quiet.

"The midges," she said. "They've gone."

"So they have," said Corvus. "That's odd."

"Well, that's as may be. But there's nothing for it, we'll have to go down," said Edric.

They readied their hunting spears and began to force their way through the undergrowth. After a few minutes they came out into an open space, clear of trees, the ground a rocky, dried-up river bed.

Nothing could have prepared them for the sight that lay before them. Ahead there was a low cave mouth and in front of it two wooden poles – poles upon which had been impaled two severed heads – the heads of Aldfrid and Aldhelm, covered in a great cloud of gnats, flies and midges. Merewyn let out a shocked cry.

"By the sleet-cold halls of Hel, that is not the work of wolves," said Corvus, aghast.

But there wasn't time to stop and stare. As if to put the lie to his words, a sudden howling filled the air. Around the edge of the hollow bowl, grey shapes appeared, looming large. Wolves. Huge wolves! Snarling, they charged down the sides of the hollow from all sides, a concerted attack, as if they'd planned it from the beginning.

"Quick," said Edric, "back to back, spears at the ready!"

The wolves closed in. The humans jabbed with spears. A wolf shrieked in pain. Another whimpered as a spearhead took it in the eye. They fell back, yapping, biting at the spear shafts, but for now they were held at bay. Then one managed to get its jaws on Merewyn's spear shaft. Instead of pulling and worrying at it like a normal wolf, it simply drew the shaft to the ground, opening up a line of attack for its pack brothers.

Two of the wolves now charged at Merewyn, their jaws gaping, looking to rip out her throat. Merewyn had to drop her spear, going for the long dagger at her belt. Corvus reached up with one hand, the other still jabbing his spear. He let fly with one of his axes, and it flew true, shattering the skull of the first wolf. Merewyn managed to get an arm up in time and the jaws of the second wolf closed with a snap on her wrist. Fortunately, it was protected by her leather archer's vambrace, giving Merewyn time to plunge her long dagger deep into the wolf's neck, severing its jugular vein. The creature fell back, spouting blood, crawling away to die.

Meanwhile Merewyn's spear had been dragged away, out of reach, as if the wolves knew its power and what it could do to them.

"Between us, get between us," shouted Edric to Merewyn. "We'll protect you with our spears – use your bow!"

The wolves circled them, snarling viciously, yellow eyes ablaze with bloodlust, looking for openings, thirsty for blood and hungry for man-flesh. But then Merewyn let fly with her bow. A wolf went down instantly, an arrow straight through the eye. Another took an arrow in the side and crawled away, snarling in pain. The rest of the pack turned on it, tearing at the dying wolf, ripping it to pieces.

That gave them a few moments of respite, during which Merewyn shot another wolf, and Corvus managed to retrieve his axe. It looked like they were getting the better of the wolves. There were only five left now.

But then something shouldered its way out of the cave mouth – a huge wolf with a heavy, shaggy pelt of mottled grey fur. Its eyes were alight with an eerie greenish glow, glittering with unnatural intelligence. It threw back its great head and howled. The other wolves snapped out of their feral rage, all eyes on their pack leader. The great beast howled again. The wolves charged – this time with uncanny purpose. One leapt at Edric, another at Corvus. They died on their spears, but in the meantime two others dashed in from either side straight at Merewyn – almost as if they knew she was the greater threat and had to be taken down first. Merewyn shot one straight through the head, but the other came in from behind and sank its teeth into Merewyn's calf. She cried out in pain and fell to one knee.

Corvus dropped his spear and wheeled. In a flash he brought his axes down, cutting off the wolf's head in a spray of blood. Merewyn gave another cry of pain, and looked up at Corvus angrily.

The wolf's teeth had tightened in death, reflexively clamping harder on her leg. Corvus made a face. "Ooops," he said.

Meanwhile Edric, without his spear, was holding the last wolf at bay, its snarling maw inches from his face.

"Some help here!" he cried.

Corvus finished it with his axes. Enraged at the death of his pack, the great grey wolf bayed at them, as if in angry admonishment. Slowly, it began to pace towards them. Merewyn was in agony, but she managed an arrow shot. It spent itself uselessly in the beast's shaggy fur, unable to penetrate so much hair. Edric, having retrieved his spear, stood over Merewyn, pointing it at the great wolf. It paused, unsure. Corvus bent down and pried open the jaws of the dead wolf's head that were locked around Merewyn's leg. It came away, and a rush of blood poured from the wound. Merewyn gasped in pain, close to fainting. Corvus threw the head aside and began tending to her leg as best he could. In the meantime, Merewyn, with a Herculean effort, managed another shot, this time at one of the wolf's legs, where the fur was thinnest. The shot went home, and the great wolf howled in pain. It turned and fled, limping, back into the cave.

Edric breathed a sigh of relief. He kept watch on the cave mouth, while Corvus ministered to Merewyn. He managed to staunch the bleeding, bandaging her leg tightly.

"Can you walk?" asked Edric. Merewyn limped to her feet. "Not without help," she said. "But I can stand."

"Well, that's better than I'd hoped," said Edric. He looked at Corvus. "We have to go in there and finish the thing," he said.

Corvus nodded grimly. "Aye," he said, "Otherwise it'll heal up and start again. Find another pack."

"King of the wolves," said Merewyn through gritted teeth. "I've never seen anything like it. Get its head. It'll make a fine trophy," she said gamely.

"We'll try our best," said Edric with a grin. Just then there was a sudden roar, as of someone bellowing in anger. Out of the cave burst a huge man, his arms and legs knotted with muscle. He wore a

244

great wolf pelt, and in one hand he held a massive wooden club. His hair was wolf-grey, hanging down his head like a lion's mane, and his eyes were ablaze with a strange, greenish light.

An arrow shaft, broken off above the head, was embedded in his leg. The three gawped at him in astonishment.

"A berserker-wolf!" said Corvus. "A shape-changer!"

"What?" said Edric.

"A man who can take on the form of a wolf! Look at his eyes – they are the same. And that arrow wound – exactly where Merewyn shot the great wolf," said Corvus, fingering his amulet and making the sign against the evil eye.

Edric stared in amazement. "It cannot be," he said. But they had no more time to debate it. The man gave another great roar and charged. Merewyn shot at him, but he batted the arrow out of the air with his free hand.

Corvus gasped. Such speed! He considered throwing his axes, but there was no point. If the wolf-man could knock an arrow out of the air, thrown axes would be child's play. The creature ran in, aiming a great blow at Merewyn. Edric thrust with his spear, but the wolf-man twisted aside with surprising agility. Corvus cut with his axes, but they could not penetrate the wolf-man's great wolf pelt, their force muffled by the voluminous fur.

The wolf-man struck Merewyn a mighty blow, sending her flying through the air. She fell unconscious to the ground. The wolf-man stepped over her, readying a crushing blow to her head, virtually ignoring the other two.

Edric ran forward, driving his spear into the ground, before vaulting into the air. He struck the huge man in the back of the neck with both booted feet. The giant grunted before stumbling forward, unable to finish Merewyn off. His feet caught in the undergrowth, and he began to teeter off balance.

Meanwhile, Corvus dove into a forward roll and came up slashing with his axes at the back of one of the wolf-man's legs. They cut deep, virtually severing his leg above the ankle. The man-beast toppled to the ground with a wailing howl that sounded more wolf than man, twisting as he landed to fall on to his back. But instantly, with a kind of feral energy, he sat up, bringing his club round in a great arc. Corvus leapt high into the air over the swinging blow. As he came down, he threw both axes with all his strength, slamming them into the wolf-man's chest. Though they did not bite – the shaggy pelt protected him – the force of the blow threw him down on to his back once more.

Edric stepped in, thrusting down with his spear. It took the wolf-man in the shoulder. Edric pushed hard, leaning all his weight into the spear, driving it down. The spear lanced through to the ground below, pinning the wolf-man to the forest floor. He snarled in raging agony, and brought his club around, knocking Edric into the air. He flew several feet and then collapsed on the ground, out like a light.

Corvus darted in and snatched up his axes. The wolf-man tried to pluck out the spear with his other hand, but he couldn't get a good grip on it, not with his shoulder pinned. Dropping the club, he reached up with that hand instead and snapped the spear in two, as if it were matchwood. Then he heaved himself up off the impaling spearhead, leaving it stuck in the ground, covered in blood. But Corvus closed in and slammed both axes together on either side of his massive neck. An ordinary man's head would have been taken off in an instant by such a strike, but not the wolf-man's.

The axes bit, blood burst forth, but the wolf-man didn't die. Instead he grabbed Corvus by the throat with both hands, eyes glowing with bright green rage, growling like a wolf. His grip tightened. Corvus choked, his eyes bulging. It was like having your neck in a vice. Desperately he drew his axes back and hacked once more at either side of the neck. It was like chopping into a side of beef. The grip on his throat actually tightened. He couldn't breathe. He hacked again. The strength was going out of his arms. He tried to hack once more but his axes fell from his nerveless fingers. His vision darkened. He was going to die, strangled by this shape-changing berserker.

But suddenly the pressure ceased. The hands fell away. Corvus drew in great gulps of air, his vision clearing. The wolf-man fell back to earth, his eyes rolling up into the back of his head. The loss of blood from neck and leg was too much, and he was dying at last, his wolf pelt drenched in gore. With a horrible shudder the great man-beast breathed his last. It was over.

Corvus sheathed his axes wearily. Thank Thor for that. He'd had his fill of wolves – two- and four-legged. He staggered over to his comrades.

Some water splashed in the face brought Edric around. He'd have a headache and some bruising, but he would be all right. Merewyn, however, was in a bad way. She had a broken arm and a nasty bite wound. While she lay unconscious, Corvus set her arm, strapping it up as best he could. He was no healer, but he had good battlefield first-aid skills.

Then he began cutting wood to make a simple wooden pallet, so they could drag Merewyn back through the forest. In the meantime, Edric investigated the cave.

He came back out after a half-hour or so, dragging a large wooden chest, a big grin on his face. Inside, it was full of silver coins and gold armbands – a vast fortune.

"We're rich!" said Corvus.

"Well, not really," said Edric. "It's the king's, as this is his expedition. But Oslac will be generous; he'll give us a good share, that's the tradition. Also, all this stuff is loot the wolf-man gathered from Oslac's people. So it is doubly the king's."

"I'm sure he wouldn't miss some… but I guess it wouldn't be right," said Corvus reluctantly.

"And I am the king's champion, Corvus. One of his most trusted men. I have a duty to the king, under oath. I couldn't allow it." He said all this in a friendly enough way, with a smile on his face, but it was obvious he meant it. Corvus flicked the hair out of his eyes and thought for a moment. He had to respect what Edric was saying. Even though Oslac wasn't his king, it still wouldn't be right.

"Oh, well," said Corvus with a sigh.

"There is something else, though," Edric said. "I found a pile of gear – leather armour, spears, a few rusty old swords, most of it rotten and useless, no doubt collected by the wolf-man from his victims. But underneath it I found this."

He took out of the chest something long and

bulky, wrapped in a small leather blanket, and laid it on the ground. Carefully he unwrapped it. The inside cover was coated in linseed oil. On it rested two beautiful axes. Each had a well-varnished, perfectly carved ashen haft and an iron ball at the end, clasped to the haft by finely fashioned silver talons, as of an eagle or raven. The axe-heads were polished steel, sharp as razors and inlaid with an engraved pattern of exquisite workmanship. Where the axe-head was fixed to the haft, a name was written in Viking runes. One axe was called 'Brainbiter', the other, 'Bloodspiller'.

Corvus gaped in astonishment. Such fine axes, and of Viking heritage! They were like axes a hero would carry at Ragnarök itself.

"They are yours," said Edric with a grin. "You deserve them. I'll see to it Oslac gifts them to you, even if I pay for it from my own share."

Corvus was speechless with gratitude. He picked up the axes, his eyes shining. How beautiful they were, how perfect.

CHAPTER 20

SIGHERE THE BALD

It was early evening of the tenth day since they'd set out when Edric, Corvus and Merewyn finally returned to Selsea. Corvus and Edric were pulling a makeshift wooden pallet behind them, upon which lay the wounded Merewyn, the chest of treasure and a sack containing the head of the wolf-berserker. The trip back had taken several days; the pallet made for slow progress.

They took Merewyn to the city hospice, run by the Nuns of St. Pegia. They knew Edric as the king's champion and took the girl in without demur. The abbess assured them that as long as no infection set in she would recover fully and be back on her feet in a few days, though it would be a lot longer before her arm healed and she could shoot a bow again.

It was too late to see the king, so Edric and Corvus found lodgings at an inn, where they ate mightily and sank a few drinks before retiring early to bed, exhausted.

The next day, they made their way to the king's hall with the chest, the sack and its grisly contents, which smelled pretty bad by now. They were recognised and ushered in. Slowly they paced down the long walkway. Up in the rafters, Corvus couldn't help noticing the hole in the ceiling he'd spotted the last time he was there. It still hadn't been repaired properly. He could hear banging and shouting from the workmen on the roof.

They approached the throne. But it was Sighere the Bald, not Oslac, sitting there. Corvus' heart sank. Beside Sighere stood the wizened priest, Oslac's chamberlain. Several Huscarls were lined up close by.

Sighere greeted them with a sardonic grin and a mocking edge to his voice. "So the great hunters have returned, eh? I hope your trip was a successful one."

Corvus and Edric drew closer. They did not kneel, nor did the chamberlain force them to. Edric said, "Where is Oslac?"

"Away," said Sighere. "Offa, the high king, has summoned him to a council meeting. It seems the king of the East Angles is causing trouble. Oslac has left me in charge. As his regent. With full authority."

Corvus and Edric looked at each other. This didn't bode well.

"And what have we here?" said Sighere, descending from the throne. Corvus picked up the sack and pulled out their grisly trophy, the severed head of the wolf-man. Sighere recoiled in disgust, holding his nose against the stink of rotting flesh, and then frowned in puzzlement.

"I thought you were hunting wolves!" he said.

Edric explained their adventures, including the death of Aldfrid and Aldhelm. Sighere was astounded. "You really believe this man was a shape-changer, a wolf-berserk?" he asked.

"It could be," said Edric. "We certainly found no trace of the great grey wolf, just this man, wounded exactly where Merewyn wounded the wolf with her arrow."

"I believe it," said Corvus. "There are many tales of the berserker rage in our land, and it is said that many of them are also shape-changers. Wolf-berserkers, or sometimes the bear."

"Oh, yes, the church has heard of this sort of thing as well, Lord Sighere," piped up the priest-chamberlain. "These wolf-men are the sons of Satan, sent here to plague good Christian folk, to terrify them and force them away from the true path! It is no coincidence that they are Norsemen, for it is well known that the men of the north are pagan barbarians, children of the evil one, come here to do the devil's work."

Sighere shrugged. "Hah, I can believe that last bit. But wolf-men? Hmm. Perhaps." He stared at the severed head, fascinated. Gingerly, he leant forward and lifted an eyelid. And then he recoiled for real, crossing himself. "By Christ," he said. "He has the eyes of a wolf!"

Corvus smiled at Sighere's discomfort, bringing a scowl of annoyance to Sighere's face.

"And this," he said, pointing at the chest, "is the berserker's loot?"

"Aye, lord," said Edric, shifting uncomfortably.

Sighere flipped open the lid and gasped. "My, what a lot of gold and silver. Of course, this all belongs to the king, you know," he said, glancing slyly over at Corvus.

"Aye," said Edric. "But it is customary to give a share to those who won it for the king."

"Indeed it is," said Sighere. "Of course! Here you are, Edric," he said. He picked up several golden armbands, a small fortune, and handed them to him.

"Thank you, my lord, you are generous," said Edric.

"Take the same for Merewyn the hunter," he said. Edric did so, and then stepped back, waiting for Sighere to do the same for Corvus.

"Nothing for the outlander," said Sighere, smirking. Edric's jaw dropped.

"But without him, we all would have

been killed! He deserves more than any of us," protested Edric.

"Nothing for the outlander!" said Sighere, louder this time. "The laws of the treasure hoard do not apply to him, for he is not a Saxon!"

Corvus raised his eyes, trying to control his anger. Still, none of it really mattered, as long as he could free his sisters. Let Sighere have his gold.

"In fact," said Sighere, stepping back and looking at Corvus, "those rather fine axes on your back, of most excellent craftsmanship…"

Corvus stared at him, blue eyes blazing. "They are mine," he said emphatically.

"Well, no, they're not, are they? In fact, they're part of this treasure hoard," said Sighere silkily. "You told me, when you were recounting your tale. Therefore they are the king's, and it is up to him what he gives and what he doesn't. And as I am the king's representative while he is away, the decision is mine. Hand them over."

Sighere smiled triumphantly and put out his hands. Corvus growled. He tossed his head defiantly and reached for his axes with lightning speed. Sighere's eyes widened, and he stepped back in fear.

"No!" said Edric. Corvus frowned, gripping the handles of his axes. The Huscarls flanking the throne stepped forward, hands on weapons.

"Corvus, calm down," said Edric. "Give him the axes."

Corvus sighed. Slowly he brought them forth and handed them over to Sighere. Oh, how he wanted to smash them into that arrogant, gloating face, to splatter his brains all over the walls. But he couldn't. Not here anyway.

Sighere took the axes, grinning like the cat that got the cream, and put them in the chest. He ordered his guards to take the chest to the king's treasury – a chamber just behind the throne.

Edric turned to Sighere and handed back his gold armbands. "I cannot accept these. If Corvus gets nothing, then I get nothing," he said.

Sighere gave a half-smile. "Oh, yes, you will accept these," he said. "I command it. And I wield the full authority of the king."

"I will not," said Edric.

"Oh, yes, you will. In fact, wear them. On your arms. Now!"

Edric shook his head once more. Sighere went right up to him, and screamed into his face, "I command it! And I wield the full authority of the king! Is that not so, priest?"

The chamberlain gulped.

"Is that not so, priest?" said Sighere again, emphasising each word, daring the chamberlain to disagree.

"Er, well, yes. Technically, that's true…" stuttered the priest.

"Technically?" said Sighere. "Either it's true or it isn't," he said, staring Edric full in the face.

"Um, it's true. Yes, of course it is. I have it written down here, a royal edict," said the priest.

Sighere smiled. "A royal edict, no less. Well, Edric?"

Edric sighed. He had no choice but to put on the gold armbands. Sighere stepped back, satisfied, and settled himself on the throne.

"Anything else?" he asked, knowing full well there was.

"My sisters," said Corvus. "Where are my sisters? I have fulfilled my part of the bargain – the king promised to free them."

Sighere grinned even more joyfully.

A muscle began to twitch in Corvus' jaw. He couldn't take much more of this. He might have to kill someone in a minute. Someone bald.

Sighere pulled himself together. "Well, you see, there's a bit of a problem with that," he said.

"Problem?" said Corvus, eyes ablaze.

"Yes, a bit of a clerical error," said Sighere.

"An error! What do you mean?" growled Corvus.

"Well, nobody told the master of slaves that these two girls were important. He saw an opportunity to make a profit for the king's household. So he sold them," said Sighere, grinning from ear to ear.

"Sold them?" said Corvus. He took a step forward, hands clenched. "I'll rip..."

"Corvus, no!" Edric said, putting a restraining hand on Corvus' shoulder. Sighere's guards stepped forward once more, hands on their weapons.

Sighere slapped the sides of the throne in glee. "Yes, sold them. To a Frankish slave trader from over the sea – ironically on the day after you left for your wolf hunt. Ten days gone – no doubt they're somewhere in Francia now. Almost impossible to find!"

"What was the name of this merchant?" said Corvus through gritted teeth.

"Dagobert," said Sighere, "from the court of King Charlemagne. Probably taken them back to him, no doubt."

"What does he look like?" said Corvus.

"Well, let me see. When I spoke to him last, as it happens, the day after you left for your wolf hunt, he looked like a typical merchant. Fat and rich. Very fat," said Sighere, laughing like a madman.

Corvus stared at Sighere with loathing. Then he turned his back on him and began to walk out. Edric turned to follow him, but Sighere shouted, "Edric Godwyn, where are you going? Come here!"

Edric ignored him. Sighere shouted even more loudly, "Edric! Remember your oath. Your Blood Oath of allegiance to the king. To protect and obey the king *and his family*. Get back here now!"

Edric paused and cursed. "Corvus," he called after him. "I'm sorry. He's right; I am bound by that oath. I have to obey."

Corvus turned and without a word, went straight up to Edric and embraced him.

"Awww, how sweet," said Sighere mockingly.

Corvus ignored him. Then he turned and stormed out of the king's hall in a towering rage, murderous thoughts running through his head, imagining all the different ways he'd like to kill Sighere. He had to get out now, before he did something rash.

He went straight to a tavern. Over a drink, he calmed himself down, thinking through his options. When he'd got hold of his temper, and come up with what he thought was a good plan, he set off through the streets of Selsea to visit Merewyn.

CHAPTER 21

A PARTING OF THE WAYS

*C*orvus rapped on the hospice door. A woman of indeterminate age, covered in white unbleached linen from head to foot, face hidden behind a veil, with a wooden cross around her neck, answered the door. Corvus stepped back for a moment. She looked like she was wrapped in a corpse shroud, as if she'd just stepped out of the grave.

"I wish to see Merewyn," he said. The woman said nothing, simply nodded and let him through. He found Merewyn in a small cell, sitting up in bed; leg bandaged and arm in a sling, being read to by a young woman.

Merewyn grinned up at Corvus. "Give us a

minute, would you, Elvina?" said Merewyn politely. The young nun left the room with a rustle of skirts, smiling at Corvus and giggling.

Corvus raised an eyebrow. "What's she laughing about?" he asked.

"Nothing, nothing at all," said Merewyn. Corvus frowned. It looked like Merewyn was embarrassed about something. Maybe even blushing. But he couldn't be sure. He wasn't very good at that sort of thing.

"So you're on the mend, then?" said Corvus, rather lamely.

"Yes, much better already after a few nights' rest. They are good healers here. What happened with the king?" she said in a businesslike way.

Corvus explained everything to Merewyn.

"That bald bastard," said Merewyn. "You should kill him!"

"I'd like to," said Corvus, "but that would put Edric in an impossible situation. He's sworn an oath to Oslac and his family. But I am going to get what's mine."

"What do you mean?" said Merewyn.

"I've got a plan," said Corvus.

"Oho! A plan, eh? The trouble is, Corvus, your

plans usually involve a lot of people ending up dead. I hope you're not planning anything like that here in Selsea," said Merewyn.

"No, it's a good plan. I don't have to kill anyone. After tonight, I'll make a run for it down the coast. Find a small village, get a boat, head to the land of the Franks and find my sisters. And then find Wulfric and fulfil my oath of vengeance," said Corvus.

"Well, in that case I'll get my stuff. Be with you in a minute," said Merewyn. As she moved to get up, she winced and gasped in pain.

"No, no! You're not well enough," said Corvus. "And it'll be dangerous, especially for you. If they catch me, well, I'm just another Viking. But you'd be a traitor, and the punishment for treason is a slow, painful death. So I've come to say goodbye," said Corvus.

"Goodbye? You can't... you..." Merewyn's eyes began to water. "You promised my father..."

"Aye, I did, but you're far safer here than with me! Wherever I go, death himself is always a few paces behind me. The Valkyries, choosers of the slain, fly at my shoulder. My fate is bloodstained, my future red. No, best you stay here."

"No! When I'm better, I'll come and find you – I will!" insisted Merewyn.

"But I'm going to Francia. Over the sea. I don't even know where I'm going to end up. You'll never find me," said Corvus.

"Oh, yes I will. I'll just follow the trail of dead bodies," said Merewyn.

Corvus threw back his head and laughed out loud. Merewyn grinned.

"I'll be looking for Charlemagne, king of the Franks," said Corvus. "If you do come, look for him too, and likely you'll find me near. It won't be hard to find a king."

Merewyn nodded. They looked at each other in silence for a moment. She put her hand out.

"One final thing," said Corvus. "I'm not going to be able to see Edric before I go. If you see him, don't tell him about my plans. It'd put him in a real dilemma. Either way he's not going to be too pleased with me. In fact, don't tell anybody I came to see you, not until tomorrow, anyway." He thought Edric might guess what he was going to do – but he didn't think the king's champion would stand in his way.

"Of course," said Merewyn.

Corvus nodded his thanks. "I'd better get going," he said.

"Goodbye, then, Corvus. I'm sorry I doubted you," said Merewyn.

Corvus took her hand and shook it. She pulled him down and kissed him lightly on the cheek. Corvus coughed, embarrassed, his cheeks reddening. Merewyn grinned, which made Corvus even more embarrassed. Fierce warrior though he was, five years in the Danish king's army had given him little experience with girls.

"Goodbye, Merewyn," he said. Quickly he changed the subject. "By the way, Edric's got your share of the spoils – a tidy sum, in fact."

Merewyn nodded. "Thanks, that'll come in handy," she said.

Corvus looked at her, not sure what to say next. "Umm, look, if you're ever in trouble, send word if you can, and I'll come find you."

With that he left.

CHAPTER 22

BRING ME THE HEAD OF CORVUS GUNNARSON!

After he took his leave of Merewyn, Corvus spent the afternoon working on his plan. He knew it was absurdly ambitious, but he wasn't going to let that cunning little swine Sighere walk all over him.

As evening closed in, Corvus took a meal at the tavern. Then he retired to his room, where he dozed until the early hours. Rising, he wrapped himself in a dark woollen cloak, pinned with the raven brooch the standard-bearer had given him. Then he took the sack of gear that he'd prepared earlier and climbed out of his window on to the deserted streets of Selsea. With a half-full moon and a cloudy sky, visibility was poor. That suited him.

As quietly as he could, Corvus made his way through the sleeping town to the king's hall. Torches sat in brackets along the portico roof, and large braziers of hot coals warmed the Huscarls at the gate. Skirting the entrance, Corvus made his way to a corner that was deep in shadow. There he reached into his sack and took out four short stubby knives. Two he fastened securely to his boots, so that the blades protruded from the end of his toes. The other two he took in his hands. Kicking a bladed boot into the wooden timbers of the hall, he hefted his weight on to it before stabbing the wood further up the wall. Then up came the other boot. *Thwock*! He drove it into the wood. Then another hand. Then he wrenched his other boot free, lifted it up higher and drove it in again. He scaled the wall like a spider, shifting his weight, praying to Thor that there wasn't someone directly on the other side of the wall who could hear him.

The gods must have smiled on him, because he crested the edge of the roof without incident. Pausing for a moment, he put away his climbing knives. Then carefully he crawled along the wooden roof until he reached the large hole he'd seen the first time he'd come to the hall and noticed again this morning. Workmen's tools were scattered around; half-finished timbers and planks were lying nearby. Thank Thor for careless workmen, thought Corvus to himself, fingering his amulet. He leant down and put his head through the hole. He could hear the faint sound of talking coming from somewhere in the hall, but nothing directly beneath him. There was a faint light coming from somewhere, but this part of the hall was pretty much shrouded in gloom. Corvus drove one of his short-bladed knives as deep as he could into the wooden roof. Then, taking a length of rope from his sack, he knotted one end on to the embedded knife, and lowered the rest of it down into the shadows.

As carefully and quietly as he could, he shinned down the rope, his heart beating like a drum. If he was found out –

He reached the bottom. There he removed his heavy leather boots, tied them together and slung them around his neck. Barefoot, he silently crept to the edge of the hall, where the shadows were deepest, and made his way towards the throne. There was no one about, though he could still hear voices coming from somewhere. They grew louder. He frowned. Why aren't they in bed, by the sleet-cold halls of Hel?

He worked his way round to the back of the throne. There were the double doors to the king's treasury. They were very tall, twice the height of a man, like the doors at the front of the hall, though these were wooden rather than iron. He'd expected a guard or two at the door, but there was no one there, which was odd.

Looking around suspiciously, alert for some kind of trap, he made his way to the doors. The voices began to get louder, and he realised the doors were slightly ajar.

Quietly Corvus stepped up to the doors, knelt and ventured a glance inside. The room was stacked with sacks, jars, jugs, bottles, boxes and chests. He saw food, weapons and money. This must be the actual treasury. At the far end of the room there was a pool of light, coming from several lanterns hanging on hooks from the low ceiling. Seated at a table were two figures, backs to Corvus. One wore a hood. The other's head was shiny and bald. Sighere! What was he doing here at this time of night, by Thor's hammer?

"How much is that?" asked Sighere.

"One hundred silver pennies, my lord," replied the hooded figure. It was the royal chamberlain, the wizened old priest.

Sighere was counting his money, the miserly skinflint. Or, rather, his uncle's money. But why at night? Ah, of course. Sighere was probably helping himself while the king was away, the greedy swine.

Corvus narrowed his eyes. Here was a chance to deal with Sighere once and for all. Killing him wouldn't be that hard, except that he'd probably have to kill the chamberlain as well. Maybe that was a bad idea; the chamberlain was an old man. He was also a priest, and killing him might anger the gods – any gods. Still... Sighere on his own... Corvus shook his head, thought better of it. He was in the king's hall. Many of the Huscarls were barracked here in various chambers off to the sides, fifty or more. They could be here in seconds.

Then Corvus caught sight of the treasure chest from the wolf-berserker's hoard. Resting on top of it were the axes, Bloodspiller and Brainbiter, no more than six feet away. Corvus looked behind him and saw no one. He looked in again. The room was dark, save where Sighere and the priest were counting coins, their backs to him. He had to go for it.

Gingerly he rose to his feet and tiptoed into the room. One step, two, three, four. He was by the chest. Beyond it was a pile of grain sacks. He stepped over the chest and crouched, shielded from view by the pile of sacks. Suddenly he felt the urge to laugh out loud. He clasped a hand over his mouth, then pinched himself hard. The urge faded.

Corvus picked up the axes. How good they felt! Such fine workmanship. He slotted them neatly into the harness on his back. Then he lifted the lid. Inside – gold, silver, just as before. He took a couple of gold armbands and fastened them around his wrists. Then a handful of silver coins, carefully, one at a time so they wouldn't jangle. When he felt he had taken a fair share, he closed the lid. It gave a tiny click. Corvus' heart leapt into his mouth. Had they heard? After a heart-stopping moment or two of panic, he began to relax. No one had heard. Sighere and the chamberlain were still talking, their voices low.

Corvus stood up and began to tiptoe back towards the door. Then he heard more voices. He froze. They were coming from the other side of the doors!

Suddenly the doors swung open, and two Huscarls walked in. They stopped, expressions of shock on their faces.

"What the..." one spluttered.

"By the holy Christ!" said the chamberlain, looking up from his coins, equally surprised.

Corvus glanced behind him. Sighere was staring at him, mouth open, eyes wide. "It cannot be..." he said disbelievingly.

Corvus smiled at him, gesturing at the axes on his back. "Just helping myself to what's mine, you mealy-mouthed, petty-minded, shiny-pated little swine," he said.

Sighere's face became an ugly mask of rage. "Get him! Get him, you idiots!" he shrieked. The guards reached for their weapons.

Corvus ran straight at them. Between him and them was a large wooden chest. Corvus leapt up on it and then used it as a springboard to hurl himself into the air, somersaulting over their heads and through the high doorway. As he sailed over, they gaped at him, still scrabbling for their weapons.

Corvus landed lightly on his feet, and ran down the great hall. Behind him came the two guards, slowed by their shields and chain mail shirts, with Sighere behind them. Corvus ran on, outstripping them easily. He darted off to the side of the hall. At regular intervals there were windows, and it was an easy matter to rip the shutters open and dive through.

Behind him he could hear Sighere raging. "Break

out the Huscarls! After him!" he screamed. This was followed by a stream of foul invective, then, "Bring me the head of Corvus Gunnarson!" Corvus grinned. He'd really got up the slime-faced toad's nose this time!

Sighere's calls for his head began to fade as Corvus made good speed through the predawn gloom, past sleepy houses and slumbering townsfolk. He paused briefly to put his boots back on and then ran for the city gates, planning to find a nearby fishing village, to rent, buy or steal a boat, then sail across the channel to the land of the Franks. From there he'd try to find Dagobert the merchant or King Charlemagne and his court – somehow. He'd have to trust to luck and the blessings of Thor.

Corvus ran at a light, steady pace, eating up the distance. He looked behind him, back at the king's hall. He could see torches, fifty or more, the light casting menacing shadows of helmets and spears on the ancient marble façade of the hall. There was going to be a pursuit.

Corvus sped up and shortly came to the Selsea city gates. He slowed to a walk, trying to get his breath back. The gates were shut, as they always were at night. Two guards sat on stools on either side, one snoring loudly, the other gazing up at the stars.

Corvus sauntered up as nonchalantly as he could, controlling his breath. The stargazing guard heard his approach and picked up a lantern.

"What are you doing up at this time of night?" he asked suspiciously.

"Are you Hengist?" said Corvus. "I'm looking for a Hengist of Chippham; apparently he's in the city watch."

The guard looked puzzled for a moment. "I don't know a Hengist. Haven't even heard of Chippham. What's he look like?" he asked.

"Well," said Corvus, leaning in. Suddenly he punched the guard right on the jaw. He fell straight back, out like a light. Corvus caught him before he hit the ground, then laid him out quietly and carefully.

Lifting the great iron bar that held the gate shut, he stepped outside, pulling it closed behind him.

Then he ran, following the road over the Selsea

Bridge and out of the town. Soon he came to a three-way crossroads. Straight ahead led directly inland. The road to the right went to the Great Forest. The road to the left followed the coast. Corvus took the coast road, running at a steady pace. Behind him, the sounds of pursuit faded into the night.

CHAPTER 23

THE WHALE ROAD

Corvus was tired, hungry and cold. He had walked through the night, along a track that led through a forest and up a steep hill. But the dawn raised new hope in his heart, for the sun's rays revealed the sea. A small village nestled on the seashore at the bottom of the hill. Fishing boats were drawn up on the sand, gulls were crying overhead. The sleepy hamlet was beginning to wake up.

Corvus walked on with renewed vigour. He could find a boat here, and food. As he neared the village, he could see smoke appearing at chimney-holes. The sun began to burn away the mists of dawn and warm his tired bones.

The little hamlet had perhaps fifteen to twenty houses. And an inn, thank Thor! Corvus was ravenous. He walked down the hill at a leisurely pace, enjoying the view, the feel of the sun warming his bones, the anticipation of a good meal, and the thought of a journey across the sea. He had plenty of money – it would be easy enough to get a huge meal and then buy a small fishing boat. His spirits lifted, but not for long.

As he neared the outskirts of the hamlet there was a sudden shout from above. Corvus spun around. Behind him he saw horsemen, at least fifteen of them! And they carried the banner of Sighere the Bald. They'd spotted him and were already spurring their mounts into action.

"By the sleet-cold halls of Hel! Why can't I get a day off from this stuff?" Corvus muttered under his breath. He heaved a great sigh, then narrowed his eyes, thinking fast. The horsemen had quite a lot of ground to catch up. He might just be able to make it to a boat before they reached him. Turning, he ran for the little village, raising a further chorus of shouts behind him as the spirit of the hunt filled the horsemen's hearts. The chase was on!

Corvus ran as fast as he could. But after an initial burst of speed he found it very hard going. His legs felt like trees, his arms like longship anchors, and he was panting heavily. He'd been on the road all night, and hadn't rested or eaten since he'd broken into the king's hall. He was exhausted. The horsemen began to gain on him significantly. This got their blood up further – there were more whoops and yells.

Corvus struggled on as fast as he could, battling the fatigue-pain building up in his legs. An agonizing stitch in his side added to his misery. As he ran past a farmhouse on the outskirts of the village, a woman with a milking pail in each hand stared at him in astonishment. It wasn't every day you saw a gigantic Viking warrior running down your street, muscles rippling, blue eyes blazing, black hair streaming behind him like a flag. The surprised look on her face would have made Corvus laugh out loud if he wasn't exhausted and being pursued by fifteen bloodthirsty Saxon Huscarls on horses.

Corvus staggered on. Behind him, the horsemen had strung themselves out, racing to see who would get to him first. One of them had taken a significant lead, with another close behind, and a fairly large gap had opened up between those two and the rest of the pack. That narrowed the odds.

Corvus began to slow down, then he stopped, hands on his knees, panting heavily, the picture of exhaustion. The lead rider gave a great cry of triumph, lifting a large one-handed axe over his head and leaning forward in the saddle, preparing to cut Corvus down. The second rider followed hot on his heels.

But Corvus wasn't *that* exhausted. As the rider neared, he staggered towards him as if helpless. The rider swept his axe at Corvus' head – but Corvus summoned up the last reserves of his energy and dove under the strike into a forward roll. The horsemen thundered past him with a frustrated cry on his lips. Corvus came out of his roll and leapt to his feet right under the nose of the following horse. Giving a great bellow, he flailed his arms wildly in the air. The horse reared back on its hind legs, whinnying in terror; cursing foully, the rider desperately tried to keep his seat. Corvus stepped to the side, grabbed the rider by the arm, and swung him out of the saddle as if he were nothing more than a bag of oatmeal. The rider flew through the air before hitting the ground with a sickening crunch. He lay there, whimpering in pain, clutching a broken arm.

Meanwhile, Corvus swung up into the now vacant saddle. Drawing one of his axes – Brainbiter – he spurred his horse forward. Behind him the rest of the Saxons shouted their outrage, but they were some way to the rear. Ahead of him the first rider had turned his horse. At the sight of Corvus he snarled in anger and spurred his horse to meet him, head to head, axe to axe! The Saxon's eyes were blazing with rage and murderous intent, glaring at Corvus, trying to intimidate him. Corvus readied Brainbiter, held back and up over his right shoulder. The horses thundered towards each other. Then Corvus grinned, a chilling, confident grin... it was too much for the Saxon. As they closed, the Saxon suddenly lost his nerve and swung to the side, galloping away as fast as he could.

There was a cry of dismay from the rest of the Saxons, followed by jeers and insults – aimed at the rider who'd shown his cowardice. But for Corvus it was an excellent result, just as he had planned, and without having to kill anyone. Best of all, no more tired-out, lung-burning, leg-hurting running – he had a fast horse instead.

Corvus was beginning to get his breath back. One last surge was all he needed. He glanced behind – good, he was beginning to outstrip them. After a few minutes he thundered on to the village high street. Women and children leapt out of the way, or stood and stared, wide-eyed. There were very few men about – no doubt most of them were already out in their fishing boats. He thundered on towards the seafront, where he could see a long quay. Only two small boats were moored there, no more than rowing boats with a simple sail. Not ideal, but enough to get him across the channel as long as there weren't any serious storms… like the one that hag-witch Kelda had sent against him and Orm. Anyway, he had no choice – it was a boat or death at the hands of a dozen Saxon warriors.

Suddenly, another horseman burst out of an alley on the right, screaming wildly at the top of his voice, a spear couched under one arm. Corvus sighed. He was so close to those boats! And he was tired and hungry. Why couldn't they just leave him alone? He looked over at the approaching rider. It was the first Saxon, the one who'd lost his nerve, the one with the really fast horse. No doubt stung by the mocking jeers of his comrades, he'd come back to have another go. And this time he had a spear, which gave him the edge over Corvus, especially in a head-on clash of horses, spear to axe. Well, best not let it get to that.

Calmly, Corvus brought his horse to a halt, reached up and drew forth his battle-brothers, Brainbiter and Bloodspiller. And waited, unmoving. The Saxon rode straight at him, spear aimed unerringly at his chest. When he was near enough, Corvus hurled Bloodspiller in a swift, fluid motion. But his throw was off, no doubt due to hunger and fatigue. His aim was true, but the wrong part of the axe landed full on the Saxon's helmet with a ringing sound like a bell being struck by a hammer. Even so, the force of the blow knocked the man off his horse. He crashed to the ground, arms and legs splayed. He was lucky – if the blade had struck the way it was supposed to, it would have shattered the helm *and* the skull beneath.

Corvus slid out of the saddle. Nearby villagers backed away. A boy stared at him wide-eyed in fear and fascination, but his mother hurriedly swept him up and darted away. As Corvus picked up Bloodspiller and sheathed it, a grey-bearded man stepped up. Corvus recognised him to be a priest of the White Christ like the one he'd seen in the village of Wotanhirst.

"You spared him," the priest said. "Risked your own life to bring him down without killing him. And you a Viking too! Was it Christ's mercy you showed?"

Corvus laughed. "By Thor's arse, no..." Corvus stopped himself. He was about to say something about how lucky the guy was, and how he never normally missed, and that he'd meant to kill him, but he thought better of it. Why not take credit for showing some mercy, he thought, even if it was an accident?

Corvus said, "Umm, well... you're right. There's no point in killing people just because you can, eh? Christian mercy and all that!"

The priest hesitated for a moment. But then he nodded, accepting Corvus' words. He walked over and knelt at the Saxon's side.

"His name is Drogo," said the priest, removing the Saxon's helmet and examining the bruise underneath. "He is one of Sighere's personal guards."

The priest looked up, staring into Corvus' eyes. "And he is my son."

Corvus stepped back in surprise. But then came the sound of thundering hooves, and the shouts of men on the hunt. The rest of the Saxon warriors would be here in minutes. Corvus ran for the quayside. A man was heading for one of the fishing boats, a net over his shoulder and a leather bag in one hand, completely oblivious to recent events. Corvus pelted past him at full speed.

"Whoa!" shouted the man, startled out of his skin. As far as he was concerned he was off for a day of fishing – the last thing he expected to see was a gigantic Viking warrior! Corvus leapt into the air, drawing his axes as he did so. He landed in the middle of the fisherman's boat, and smashed his axes down, splintering the hull like matchwood. The little boat began to fill rapidly with water, sinking fast.

"My boat!" spluttered the fisherman. Corvus leapt back on to the quay, landing in front of the fisherman, who stepped back in fear. Corvus thrust his head forward into the fisherman's face – causing him to quake in terror – and said, "Sorry about that, had to be done."

Then he raced off towards the other boat, as the Saxon horsemen came thundering in. They saw Corvus and hurtled towards him.

Hurriedly, he unmoored the little boat and leapt aboard. Turning, he sat, readying the oars. There was no time to raise the sail, and in any case, there was no wind. As he was about to start rowing, he looked up. The priest stood at the quay, looking at him accusingly.

Corvus looked back. "What?" he said angrily.

The priest just pointed to the rapidly sinking boat.

Corvus raised his eyes heavenward. The priest had a point, he thought to himself. These were poor people, fisherfolk. These boats were important to them. With an eye on the Saxons, he reached into his belt pouch and drew forth one of the gold armbands he had liberated from Sighere's treasure, and tossed it over to the priest. Then he started rowing. Fast.

The priest picked up the armband with wide eyes. Looking up at Corvus, he blessed him with the sign of the cross, for the armband was worth ten times the value of both boats.

Corvus rowed on, grateful for the priest's blessing. Never turn down the favour of a god, no matter which one! He saw the priest tuck the armband into his robes as the riders galloped up to the quay, shouting in frustration. The only other boat had been scuttled; their prey was getting away, and there was nothing they could do about it.

Corvus laughed, as he slowly pulled further and further away. The Saxon village began to get smaller in the distance. Corvus began to pull less often. A wave of nausea came over him. He was so tired.

There was no wind and he didn't relish the idea of rowing all the way across the channel. When the shore had faded to a stub of dirt on the horizon, he stopped and examined the forward storage hatch. Much to his relief, he found a jug of water and a leather pouch. He opened it – fish. Salted fish. Still, better than nothing. And there was a fishing line, so he'd be all right for the journey. He wolfed the fish down, followed by half of the water, and began to feel much better.

Corvus began to row again, praying to Thor for a breeze. And then it was as if Thor answered him. A southerly wind blew up, growing in strength. Corvus shipped the oars and raised the sail. The boat shot forward, cutting a path through the waves.

Corvus sat aft, hand on the tiller, thinking things over. He had to find Dagobert the Frankish merchant. He had his sisters or would at least know of their fate. And what of Wulfric and his strange companion, the standard-bearer? Corvus fingered the silver raven brooch on his cloak. What could it mean?

But such thoughts soon passed. He had his axes, Brainbiter and Bloodspiller, and his leather pouch still had plenty of coin in it, even after giving away one of his gold armbands. The salt-tang of the sea filled his nostrils, and the wind blew in his hair, sending it fluttering back like raven wings on either side of his head. Briny sea-spray splashed his face, invigorating him with its cold freshness. His heart began to soar; his spirits lifted. He was on the whale road once more, voyaging into an unknown future. Who knew what great adventures lay ahead?

GLOSSARY

Old Norse and Saxon words and their
meanings in modern English

ASGARD

The home of the Norse gods. Valhalla is in Asgard.

AESIR

One of the two groups of gods in Norse mythology,
the other and less well known being the Vanir. The
two groups are described as having waged war against
one another in the Æsir-Vanir War, resulting in the
unification of the two into a single tribe of gods.

BLOOD EAGLE

A Viking method of torture and execution. It was
performed by cutting the ribs of the victim near
the spine, breaking the ribs so they resembled
bloodstained wings and pulling the lungs out. Salt was
sprinkled in the wounds. Yuk!

CHARLEMAGNE

Charlemagne, meaning 'Charles the Great' (AD 747–814) was king of the Franks. He expanded the Frankish kingdoms into a Frankish empire that incorporated much of western and central Europe. During his reign, he conquered Italy and was crowned *Imperator Augustus* by Pope Leo III in AD 800 as a rival to the Byzantine emperor in Constantinople.

DAGR

The Norse god of the day, from which we get our modern word 'day'.

DANEGELD

Tribute paid to the Vikings to make them go away, or stop burning, raiding and pillaging. A bribe, basically. Literally 'Danish gold'.

DRENG

A young Viking warrior.

FENRIS WOLF

In Norse mythology, Fenrir or Fenrisulfr is a wolf, the son of Loki and a giantess. Fenrir is bound by the gods, but is ultimately destined to grow too large for his bonds and swallow Odin whole during the battle of Ragnarök. He also bit off the hand of Tyr, the Norse god of war.

FOREST OF ANDRED
In early Anglo-Saxon times, the forest was said to have been 190 km (120 miles) long. In the early Middle Ages, it stretched from Andred (Pevensey Castle) in East Sussex to the Dorset-Hampshire border – including what is now the New Forest.

THE FRANKS
A Germanic tribe that invaded the Roman Empire and settled in what is now Gaul in about AD 350. Over the years they forged an empire, which eventually became modern France.

FYRD
The Anglo-Saxon army, a levy of peasant farmers, raised in times of war.

GUNNARSON
Corvus' second name. Viking surnames were always

taken from the father's name. Gunnarson is literally 'the son of Gunnar'. If you were female, it'd be 'Gunnarsdottir', or 'Gunnar's daughter'. Gunnar itself means 'war-warrior'.

HEL
In Norse mythology, Hel (sometimes Anglicised or Latinised as 'Hela') is the ruler of Hel, as well as the name of the place over which she rules, the Norse underworld, the land of the dead. Hel's hall is named Eljudnr.

HUSCARLS
Elite household troops of a Saxon earl or king. A full-time permanent standing army and consequently much better trained than the *fyrd*, though much smaller in number.

JARL
A Viking word for a chieftain. Similar to the Saxon word 'earl'.

JORMUNGAND
Jormungandr, the world serpent or Midgard serpent, is

a sea serpent that became so large it could encircle the earth. It was the arch-enemy of Thor.

KNARR
A type of Viking merchant ship, built in a similar way to a longship, but slower and with more cargo space.

LOKI
The trickster god of Norse mythology. Usually a villain.

MERCIA
An Anglo-Saxon kingdom. It was centred on the valley of the River Trent and its tributaries in the region now known as the Midlands. Mercia's neighbours included Northumbria, Powys, the kingdoms of southern Wales, Wessex, Sussex, Essex and East Anglia.

MJOLNIR
The hammer of Thor. In Old Norse it literally means 'crusher'.

NJALL'S SAGA
This Icelandic epic from the 13th century describes the progress of a series of blood feuds, ending with the

burning of Njall's (a Viking who lived in Iceland) hall.

NJORD
Norse god of the sea. One of the Vanir.

NORNS
The three Norns were the weavers of the fates of men and gods, weavers of their 'Skein of Destiny'.

NOTT
The Norse goddess of the night. She was the mother of Dagr. It became our modern word for night.

ODIN AND WOTAN
Odin was the Norse king of the gods in Asgard; Wotan was the Saxon equivalent.

OFFA
The powerful king of Mercia, AD 757–796.

RAGNARÖK
In Norse mythology, this is the final battle at the end of time when the gods will fight against the giants and the forces of chaos, the Fenris wolf, the world serpent

and so on. Asgard will fall, the gods will be slain, but out of the chaos will rise a new race of men.

SCRAMSEAX
A Saxon single-edged knife.

SKALD
A Viking bard or poet.

SKJALDBORG
Literally in Old Norse 'shield fort'. Warriors would form a 'fort' by interlocking their shields, either in a 'wall' (a line of men) or, in times of a desperate defence when you were surrounded, a circle or square.

SUSSEX
Land of the South Saxons. Essex was the land of the East Saxons, Wessex the West Saxons and Middlesex, the middle Saxons.

TAMESIS
Old Saxon name for the River Thames.

THOR

the Norse god of thunder. He carried a magic hammer, Mjolnir.

THRALL

A Viking slave.

TYR AND TIW

Tyr is the Norse war god, Tiw is his Saxon equivalent.

ULFRSHEIM

Norse for 'wolf's-home'; Wulfric's settlement.

ULLR

An ancient god of the north, the god of duels and blood feuds.

VALHALLA

A great hall in Asgard, ruled by Odin. Those heroes who die in battle are taken to Valhalla (the hall of the slain) by the Valkyries, to fight with Odin at Ragnarök, the battle at the end of time.

VALKYRIE

In Norse mythology the Valkyries (Old Norse *Valkyrja*, 'choosers of the slain') are female deities who serve Odin. The Valkyries' purpose is to determine the victors of battles and wars, and to choose the most heroic of those who have died in battle for Valhalla.

VAMBRACE

Leather or metal forearm guard. Archers often wear bracers, a kind of vambrace, to strengthen their wrists and protect them from the snap of the bowstring.

VANIR

Vanir is the name of one of the two groups of gods in Norse mythology, the other and more well known being the Æsir. The two groups are described as having waged war against one another in the Æsir-Vanir War, resulting in the unification of the two into a single tribe of gods.

WHALE ROAD

A poetic term used by Anglo-Saxons and Vikings for the sea.

WHITE CHRIST
The Old Norse term for Jesus Christ, before the
Vikings themselves converted to Christianity.

WIND-WEAVER
What the Vanir, a race of Norse gods, called the sky.

WOTANHIRST
Means 'wooded hill of Wotan' in Anglo-Saxon. Wotan
was the Saxon or Germanic version of Odin, the king of
the gods. Hirst/hurst means 'wooded hill' in old Saxon.

DON'T MISS

CORVUS'

NEXT ADVENTURE

FURY OF
THE VIKINGS